The Storyteller
Inspired by a True Story

978-0-9951516-2-8

PROLOGUE

I have a very dark secret that has been eating me from within for the longest time, and I have decided to break free from it as I share my story. I hope you, as my reader, will release me from the embarrassment and shame that I have been faced with ever since a group of cold hearted storytellers intruded into the contented and peaceful life I once enjoyed.

I wish this entire episode were merely a nightmare. It began on the 7th month of the Chinese Lunar Calendar. According to the Chinese belief, the 7th month is also regarded as the Month for the Hungry Ghost, where all the orphaned evil spirits would escape the gates of hell and head up to Earth to haunt low spirited humans.

In exchange for seeking these evil spirits' empathy to ensure they do not disrupt our lives, the Chinese light joss sticks, and incense, burn offerings in the form of paper and cardboard that have been manufactured to resemble luxury items. These luxury items range from expensive chauffeured driven cars to fashion accessories such as Chanel bags, to Macbook, tablets and iPhones. Besides offering high end material things, they burn billions of 'hell money' as a symbolism to satisfy the cravings of these Hungry Ghosts.

The description of what happens during the 7th month of the Chinese Lunar Calendar is a reflection of what the storytellers are like as they hunt down vulnerable victims with low self-esteem who lack confidence in themselves. In my case, it had nothing to do with my self-esteem, but more to do with a business transaction that had gone south.

ONE
Rise & Fall

February 27th, 2015, 3:30pm PST

Jamie was working at her desk and almost done for the day. She looked out of the window and noticed the beautiful sunrays shining. The scene at Gastown looked so inviting with pedestrians walking along the side path. Everyone looked so happy and relaxed, elevating her mood as she started steering towards a more calming mode. She finished typing the final bits of her report punching in the last keystroke before looking to her tall, 30-year-old and pretty faced gay colleague, Jonathan, who was sitting right next to her in the staff room. "Yes!" she exclaimed. "It's almost time to leave for the weekend!"

"Someone's feeling cheerful and excited about the weekend, eh?" Jonathan interjected as he struck up a casual conversation with her. "So, what are your plans for the weekend?" he asked curiously.

Jamie cried excitedly with her eyes wide opened, "I'm going on a rendezvous with my dream guy tonight.... NOT!" Then admitted pathetically in a dreggy tone, "What else do you think will I be doing apart from the usual chores at home and taking the twins to their activities? That's basically what my life revolves around." Jamie sighed and banged her head down on her desk, confirming to Jonathan what a loser she was.

She would return to her spacious, classy yet rowdy house in Coquitlam, 45 minutes east of Vancouver downtown, to attend to her 12-year old bouncy and energetic twins, Russell, and Raymond. Her life seemed monotonous as it revolved around work and her kids, chauffeuring them from one activity to the next during the weekends and working at a day job weekdays to make ends meet.

The boys had been brought up well by her in a traditional Asian way where they were disciplined in all aspects, and had been taught to stay ahead in life from a tender age, to be as competitive as possible, and they were expected to set high standards for themselves. They were the only ones who understood what Jamie had been through with their father, who used to control all of them, yet had been overly reliant on her to bring home the bacon. Jamie and the boys couldn't tolerate his domineering behavior and one day she bravely called it quits. Ever since the divorce, she decided to give the boys a new lease on life, so they chose to move to Canada. She had never found the courage to date anyone else after she left her ex-husband, and had resorted to believing that no one would ever want her especially upon discovering she was a mother of two very active twins.

Jonathan asked Jamie if she had ever used any online dating sites. Jamie explained that she once signed up for an account with Ashley Madison just out

1

of curiosity, but got catfished and almost scammed by a guy by the name of Douglas whom she had met through that online dating portal. "He had a pretty face and on the first day he got to know me, he wanted us to leave the Ashley Madison portal, citing he hated the site as it was infested with too many sex deprived people. We started chatting on Google, then Viber, WhatsApp on the phone and on Skype. I realized the relationship was going too fast and over a brief time to get to know each other, he was always talking about his pathetic life. I began getting suspicious of the guy when he told me his late father had left him an apartment in the UK, and he needed to pay the property and inheritance taxes to the lawyer in the UK to transfer the title over to him." Jamie went on to tell Jonathan the whole encounter with pretty face scammer and how his voice didn't match his looks when he called her to speak over the phone. "He sounded like an African American. When we Skyped, he claimed his webcam was damaged, and so I never got the chance to see his face except from his photos."

Back in April 2013, she had shared the whole story with her best friend, Tammy, when they met for lunch at the Cactus restaurant. About how finally, after 2 months, she decided to drop the guy after his third attempt trying to 'extort' money from her. Tammy was the same age as Jamie, and a single parent too. They met 3 years ago through their children at school. At that time, Tammy was going through a divorce and had shared about her potential difficulty looking for help after school to pick up her daughter, Michelle, because she couldn't get off work until 5 in the evening. Jamie offered to pick up Michelle since she had to get her kids after school too, and agreed to care for Michelle till Tammy picked her up after work each day. Tammy had always been grateful to Jamie for the kind gesture. Over time, Jamie had started confiding in Tammy since she was new to Canada.

While dining at the restaurant during their girl's day out that same day, Tammy gave Jamie a list of good pointers to look out for when connecting with potential dates online. The list contained what she had learned through friends who were victims of online romance scams.

"Girlfriend, let me forewarn you about these scumbags," Tammy told her friend confidently.
"Rule # 1. If he has a pretty face that looks too good to be true, just drop him, girlfriend. You don't wanna be catfished. By catfish I mean he uses someone else's photos as bait to hook you. And he'll create some fictitious character as he dupes you.
Rule #2. If he claims he has fallen in love with you, that should sound an alarm. Nobody falls in love instantly, especially when they have never met face to face.
Rule #3. The smarter and more patient scammers will play the game slowly. So be on your guard. If he starts showing signs of being a loser, like telling you he needs funds for some kinda crisis, just drop him and run far, far away.
Rule #4. If they are always stationed far away from you and claim they want to meet you soon, be wary of those cause the majority of them are fake.
Rule #5. Never ever send them a single cent. They are ruthless, cold hearted bastards who will bleed you dry."

2

Jamie had locked up those rules in her mind ever since she had that conversation with Tammy. She shared the same pointers with Jonathan and told him she had always been wary of online romance scams.

"As long as you remember those rules your best friend shared with you, I don't think there is anything to be afraid of my dear," Jonathan reassured her. He Introduced Tinder and assured her he frequently used the app and "because there is a function in Tinder where you will know approximately how far you are from the other person you have been matched with, you can decide for yourself if you wanna meet him or not." Jonathan added, "Besides, the best thing about Tinder is if you are not interested in the profile of the other person, you swipe his photo to the left, and that will be the last time you get to see him because you will never be matched with him."

Hmm... no harm trying it out to kill the next 15 minutes of my time before I get off work! She thought downloading the Tinder app on her phone and linking it to her Facebook profile pictures before starting to fill out her profile.

Me: Happy gal....IOLO so I want to make the best out of my life!
Entrepreneurial, independent, self-sufficient and living life to the fullest. Fun loving, compassionate and generous... loves dogs and kids, but allergic to cats.

You: Someone Tinder-licious to fill the loneliness in her life... ambitious, fun loving with a great sense of humor... loves the outdoors, movies or watching sports.

Matched only if you are Tinder-Licious!!! Who knows? We might be Tinderized!

That should do... Ha! If only Tinder would pay me for coming up with these snazzy lines" Jamie thought to herself.

After completing her chores that evening, she sat by the window in her room and started going through profiles of potential matches. From her window, she got a magnificent panorama of Coquitlam city that stretched further southeast overlooking the snowcapped mountains - Mt Baker and Mt Rainier. That part of her house had always been her sanctuary to unwind before retiring for the night. It was also a place she would meditate or work on her planks. For an estimated 40 profiles that she viewed, she only swiped an average of 2 times to the right. Soon she felt tired and decided to log out of the app and retire for the day.

She started going through Tinder on a daily basis, usually around the end of the day before heading to bed. Along the way she was matched with a couple of guys living in BC, got to know them a little, then stopped communicating when neither party had anything else in common to talk about. One of the matches caught her attention, and that got her interested to connect with him. Brad, a father of two, recently divorced and just returned from Asia. They got along quite well chatting about their interests after noticing that they had so many things in common. She didn't want to hide that she had children from him, so she told Brad about them, and that she was supporting them single handedly, he disappeared and unmatched her from Tinder instantly. *It's ok, I was expecting this anyway. Come on, Jamie, what doesn't kill you makes you stronger!* She consoled herself once again trying to keep in mind that she really shouldn't put too much hope into Tinder or any other sites. She should just continue to play along with the app. From then on she decided she should just take the site as well as whomever she encountered with a pinch of salt. Just as kids listened to bedtime stories every night, swiping profiles to the left or right became a bedtime routine for her.

TWO
Having It All

Jamie joined her colleague, Jonathan, for lunch at a restaurant near their workplace. They entered a small restaurant with a nice quiet ambience playing soft rock music in the background.

"So how's Tinder? Are you matched with the man of your dreams yet?" Jonathan asked Jamie curiously, his eyes brimming with excitement.

"Not a single match worth talking about. But hey, I'm going to be a rich mama soon cos I'm gonna pick up the cheque from the proceeds of my house. I have sold my home and hope to reinvest my funds elsewhere. That reminds me, I need to make an appointment with my financial planner."

As she was talking about what she intended to do with her money, she started texting her friend who worked as a financial planner.

"Hey, let me know if you do learn of any good places to invest your money. I would like to park mine somewhere too," Jonathan reminded her not to leave him out of a great investment opportunity if she knew of any.

"For sure, good things need to be shared all the time!" Jamie assured her friend.

March 4th, 2015, 4.30am PST

It was another beautiful spring morning as Jamie woke up to her usual routine. She glanced out at Lafarge Lake across from her deck and noticed the resemblance of a green diamond nestling on Mother Nature's hand. She turned on the oven to prepare lunch for her kids' and herself, then returned to her sanctuary and commenced her fitness plan for the next 20 minutes, her *Bose* radio automatically came alive at 6am greeting her with the news in the background.

Still, as positive as ever, she always had the notion that each new day brought with it a brighter present when one was able to wake up healthy and happy. She always felt inspired enriching herself with one quote a day. She stood on her deck to breathe in the fresh air, overhead and in the background, an exodus of banished birds appeared as though out of a Celtic fairy tale, and she smiled as she commenced her day.

Suddenly, her phone beeped to a familiar tone alerting her of a new text message, curious, she picked up the phone to check who might have texted her at 5:30am, *"Good morning, sunshine!",* her face lit up with a grin.

Her close friend, David Smith, was finally back from his month long vacation in Europe. David, who happened to be 10 years Jamie's senior had always been her strong confidant. They met when Jamie first landed in Canada and found her first job as an operations manager with a franchised eatery. David frequented the restaurant a lot because his company had a building he was assigned to construct in that same location, and he became Jamie's first true friend in Canada. Though David and Jamie seemed to connect perfectly together, neither wanted to get past the friendship level because he had been going through a separation for a while and had issues progressing the divorce because of his two children. For the past 4 years, they had managed to keep their friendship platonic, and David would always be there whenever Jamie needed his help. Whether it was for a broken pipe under her bathroom sink, or to stage her home, he would always get those issues resolved. He even got his name under the kids' school emergency contact in the event Jamie couldn't be reached.

"Any new events happened in your life, sweet?" David was fond of addressing her with the pet name 'sweet'. Jamie related about her experience on Tinder, and that she was matched with people that she wouldn't want to spend her leisure time with.

"Please tell me you'll run far, far away if you encounter that Douglas fellow again!" replied David and added, *"I don't think you should get involved with all these online dating portals or even have anything to do with stuff like Google, or Yahoo. Just be on the safe side, sweet."*

"It can't be that bad. You are just paranoid, my dear!" Jamie joked back.

"Whatever!" And that was the final text she received from him.

***

THREE
Fast Forward
May 1st, 2015

Jamie awoke to the smell of damp cotton as if she had slept on a wet blanket. As she tried to pull the cloth from her face, she realized her hands were bound behind her back, her heart started to leap out of her chest as a jolt of adrenaline flashed through her body, she could breathe but it was pitch black, and her head was pounding with a four alarm headache. She thought she could see a light out of her right eye but quickly realized the light was in her head, it came from the pain. She bolted upright as if to stand up and discovered the chain tied to her bindings. She tugged hard, but the jolt it gave her confirmed it was securely fastened to the wall she was lying beside. She screamed in panic hardly able to breathe from the panic that had set in, she was hyperventilating while the headache was getting worse, she started losing any feeling in her arms and legs and felt as if she was about to throw up when darkness consumed her. She wilted to the floor in a heap and lost consciousness. She awoke to the sensation of light and heard a door open and footsteps approaching her, she screamed "Help me, Help,"

"Shut the fuck up bitch!" came the words from a deep voice with a distinctly African accent. Horrified, she started hyperventilating and was quickly overcome with the nauseous feeling that she was about to vomit. Suddenly, the hood over her face was stripped away, and she folded forward emptying the contents of her stomach on the floor in front of her.

"You're cleaning that shit up!" came the voice, Jamie rolled her head sideways on the floor and looked up to see a large overweight black man standing over her holding the dark blue pillow case that had been over her head. She could not reconcile the man's T shirt that said 'have a nice day' with her surroundings. Everything just made no sense, then she paused and thought to herself, *somethin... ...something doesn't fit.* She rolled onto her back and looked at the ceiling of the freezer. *Ok, I'm in a freezer.* Still, she could not grasp what was going on. The fear was fading and quickly being replaced with confusion. Where was she? What was going on?

"Why are you here?" came the voice.

She looked around as if there might be a third person in the room. The name was unfamiliar to her, she looked at the man who was asking her to explain what she was doing here.

What the fuck! She thought, *Why is he is asking me?* She stared at the ground for a minute trying to piece together what was going on but the pain in her head came rushing back like a landslide as the vision in her right eye got worse. She started to fall forward. Her body had given in to the sudden onrush of pain in her head and eye. She felt the firm, warm grip of the big man's hand holding her face as she fell forward. For a second the warm hand made her feel a little more secured. Then terror returned, and she reeled back up to pull away the man's hand, inadvertently throwing her head back and colliding with the wall she was chained to, that was it. She blacked out the second her head hit the wall.

Jamie woke to the sensation of a cool breeze across her cheeks, her hand clutched a white sheet. She was lying on her left side, her right eye could not make out where she was or what was going on around her, she rolled her head back to see the ceiling of a room, her arms and legs told her she was lying in a bed she heard the sound of a chair move and bare feet running across a wood floor.

"Jas, she's awake!" the voice was from a small boy who had been sitting by her bedside.

"Thirsty... God, I'm thirsty," she thought, then a big overweight black man entered the room, she looked at him.

"Water," she struggled pleading while trying her best to catch her breath, "water."

He said nothing and turned away coming back moments later with a plastic cup full of water. She grabbed the water from his hands like a drought parked person lost in the desert might have done. The water felt good,

"More, need more, please," she said after gulping every drop in the small plastic cup.

Jas walked out of the room and came back with another cup. Once again, she grabbed it and downed it as fast as the last one, then started to choke a bit from drinking it too fast.

"What time is it?" Jamie asked as if late for work or something. Jas just looked at her as if bewildered by her question, she saw a mirror on the wall behind him. She stood up quickly to look at herself, but it had been too fast, and she staggered catching herself on the dresser beside the bed. She looked into the mirror and saw a tall, slim woman with black hair, brown eyes and skin that would have belonged to someone thirty or so. She turned sharply to look behind her at the woman she saw in the mirror, but realized there was no one behind her. She looked directly into the one eye she had that could see clearly and exclaimed, "That's me?" Very confused and bewildered Jamie tried to piece together where she was, who she was or what events had brought her to here before she went to bed.

"Wow, what happened last night?" she questioned rhetorically.

"You hit your head," came the answer from Jas.

"What?"

"We found you in an alley, don't you remember?"

Crap, I don't remember anything, she thought to herself.

She looked back at her sheets and crumpled them up to her face to smell them as if somehow it would bring back her memory but nothing. She looked out the window and saw a busy street, but again nothing familiar. She sat down on the bed and listened to the air passing through the open window, the noise from the street, the creaking of floorboards in the room beyond as a pair of small bare feet passed over them. Then realized how completely unfamiliar everything seemed, the sounds, the smells, this man, but nothing about it seemed familiar.

"What's your name?" Jas asked softly as if in disbelief of her condition.

Jamie stared at the floor for a moment, but couldn't bring any name to mind, *Carol*? She thought, but the name was not familiar. It was just the first thought she had when Jas asked the question. She looked at the man's questioning gaze, shrugged her shoulders and replied, "I don't know, Carol maybe?"

"Wow, that was a big knock on the head, I guess."

Carol, who she now thought she was, reached behind her head to feel the massive lump at the back of her head and looked at the bloodshot right eye of that unfamiliar face in the mirror, "Oh yeah! That's a big one all right," she said while tenderly palpating the bruise and scars on the back of her neck. *Wow, must have been hit by a baseball bat,* she thought to herself, *That's bad.*

"No purse?" Jas asked.

"What?" Jamie replied, not quite catching what he just said.

"You did not have a purse?" he said, "So, it looks like you were mugged then robbed. Do you remember anything?" Jas looked intently at her asking himself, *Is she really this stunned?* He had never seen anyone lose their memory before, so he was skeptical and wondered if she could be faking it. Then he thought about her reaction and fear in the freezer the last time she awoke and compared it to her calm and relaxed composure now. *No,* he thought, *not even our best scammer could pull that off, must have been when she knocked herself out in the can. That and the trauma must have caused amnesia, but for how long?*

Jas' mind started to wonder for a minute, *She could make for a really good score in the short term if this amnesia thing sticks long enough.* He pondered for a minute how he could set her up with a new identity and use her as a decoy in his own scam for a change, he was so sick of always getting such a small share all the time with Rachel and the Syndicate, *Fucking tired of getting stuck in a revolving door.*

"The police," Carol announced, "why don't we just call the police?"

Instantly, whatever Jas was wondering about evaporated, *Fuck there is always some shit. Why would this be any different?* "You obviously don't have a clue," he replied.

"What?" she asked.

"People around here don't go to the police for anything," he explained, "cos they'll end up dead faster that way. Police here are very corrupted, and where we found you, there was also a dead body."

"What!" Carol exclaimed.

"Sorry," said Jas, "I didn't want to upset you." Jas studied Carol closely to see how she reacted to this information. She shrugged her shoulders, "Whew," she said, taking a deep breath, "food... I could use something to eat right now. What do you have?" she asked.

"Jose," shouted Jas, and the sound of small bare feet came running toward them. A small black boy of about 5-years-old wearing a T-shirt with colored stripes going horizontally around his waist, entered and paused beside Jas for instruction, then looked at Carol briefly, "What do we have in the pantry?" asked Jas,

"Still, some guava's left from last night," the boy informed.

"Ok with you?" Jas asked, turning to Carol.

"Yes, that would be fine. Thank you," she replied.

10

FOUR
Jamie is dead

Rachel checked up on Jamie's background using whatever clues she could get from her purse. "Shit, I knew it… she was one of our targets, fuck. How the hell did she clue in?" Rachel sat back for a minute to think through the implications then picked up her phone and called Jas. He replied and explained how Jamie thought she was Carol after suffering amnesia from the blow on her head.

"Well, at least that's some good news!" said Rachel, "Don't let her out and don't let anyone talk to her at all till I get back to you."

"Got it!" said Jas as she hung up the phone. The phone rang immediately after that. It was David from Germany. "Malley has been arrested at the branch on the west coast, while he was trying to withdraw from the account," he said in a calm tone.

"What the fuck did that shit do?" she asked.

"Apparently, he went off on the manager when she started to ask some questions about some large deposits made from Canada by some woman named Jamie. Do you know anything about this?" he asked, "Rachel?"

She paused to connect the dots, 'Canadian woman, here in town following the young boys and account problems in Germany at the same time. Fuck,' she said to herself, "something's up," Rachel told David to chill out, leave Malley to the Police and to get away from whatever that was going on. She promised she would call him back, but cautioned him to stay low for now and keep her informed and updated with any news.

Rachel buried her face in her hands for a minute to think through her options. She picked up the phone again, "Bill, it's Rachel we've got an issue with the account in Germany. I don't have details yet, but divert funds elsewhere for now and shut down all links."

"Ok, you've got it– Done!" said Bill promptly and hung up.

Jose turned and disappeared from the room for a moment, a few seconds later he returned waving a guava in his hand toward Carol. She grasped the fruit and took a deep bite, it was very ripe - over ripe, just at that point where all the juice ran trailing from each side of Jamie's mouth, "Oops, do you have a paper towel?

This is quite good," she said, "but very ripe." Jas nodded to Jose who darted off and was back in a moment with what appeared to be a washcloth of a sort, "Is it clean?" asked Carol.

"Clean enough!" emphasized Jas. Carol was taken aback a little with the obvious attitude displayed by Jas but didn't give it much more thought. "That was good," she thought.

Jas leaned over to Carol and said "Now, what are we to do with you, you know we are poor and with the police here as they are, there is very little we can do to help you cause as you might have figured out money is a dilemma for us. I do have a way we could help each other, though," Carol eyes him thoughtfully, *This is feeling a bit off, but all things don't seem to add up much at the moment anyway,* she thought to herself.

"Ok what's up?" she asked, "What is it you're talking about?"

"Look I don't know where you're from or what you do there, but here we have to make a living any way we can," Jas went on to say. He looked intently at Carol wondering how this might work if he just went into discussing a scam as if it were as basic as planting daisies, maybe in her condition she might just take it as breathing air or go off the handle, not really sure he thought to himself, then he heaved out "Ah hell with it if it doesn't work. I'll just whack her outside the head, and that will be the end of it."

"You could help me to help Jose the little boy, cause if we can make enough money together on this thing we can send him back to his grandma with that money and he could get to school where he belongs, not here in this terrible place." Carol nodded, *Little wrong with that,* she thought,

"Ok, what do I do?"

"Just come with me," said Jas as he got up and beckoned her out of the room.

Rachel dialed her cell phone. "Jas, is she still with you?"

"Yes," replied Jas.

"What's she like right now?"

"She thinks her name is Carol and has no memory."

Rachel asked if this was just an act and Jas told her of the events after she woke up. Rachel warned Jas to watch her carefully as she was key to getting the account in Germany unlocked and she told Jas to keep Carol very close and to report any changes in her condition.

Back in the office, Rachel had a phone call to make.

"Bill, it's Rachel again, I have the woman who caused the German bank to freeze our account in Germany, but there is a complication, she seems to be suffering from amnesia, at least for now anyway,"

Bill explained that after he had closed the other accounts out, he called in a lawyer to deal with Malley's situation. "I got through to Malley," said Bill, "and told him to keep Mum while the lawyer gets his bail sorted out. So, looks like we have contained the damage to the west coast account. The other money has already been moved," Bill explained. "I'm not sure the actual amount frozen in the account on the German west coast, but I am having the lawyer run that down. He figures, approximately several hundred thousand got locked."

Rachel paused, then said, "Ok, that's not good, though not a disaster, can we get to it?" she asked.

"No," Bill replied. "It's under investigations now by Interpol and German police. There is even some mention of Singapore."

"Christ, that's fucked up," said Rachel, "It's too much to walk away from. You know what happens if other branches of the Syndicate catch wind of this."

"No shit," said Bill, "That's why I jumped on it so fast to get a lid on it."

"Is there any way to get the office to help with this?" Rachel asked Bill.

"You aren't that stupid, Rachel," said Bill

"Neither am I and won't even make such suggestions again," said Bill.

"All right," said Rachel. "You get a grip on Germany, and I will go work on this bitch to see what shakes out."

***

Jas closed his antiquated flip phone after his brief chat with Rachel, looked at Carol and said "This way," as he pointed to the stairs visible in the hallway through the open front door of the apartment.

FIVE
Time for Role Play

"**Where are we** going?" asked Carol.

"Time to get to work," replied Jas.

"Work?" Asked Carol curiously.

"We are going for a little training."

"Training?"

"Listen," said Jas, "I told you, I would help you out right? But in return, I need your help on some things not the least of which is money."

"Shouldn't I see a Doctor?" blurted out Carol,

"Probably," said Jas. "Do you have medical insurance?"

"How the heck would I know?" replied Carol, "I'm not even sure who I am."

"Precisely," said Jas. "So, let's get to the money making part and maybe we can pay for a doctor after,"

 They both clumped and clunked their way down the old painted wooden stairs inside the old apartment building as they make their way to the main door a few floors below.

Feels muggy and hot. Carol thought to herself as they walked down the stairs. "Hey, what about Jose? We can't just leave him alone?"

Jas looked at Carol and studied her for a second or two, he had taken notice that Carol seemed to have an affinity for the young boy.

Sort of a Mom thing. He figured, and he mentally decided to play into her concern for the boy, *This could work as leverage.* He would need to create a story to get her to buy into the scam if she was going to be of any use at all.

The three of them were in tow walking down the street toward what appeared to be a small strip mall with half a dozen shops in it, each of them laden with graffiti and heavy bars on the windows. They came up to a small pizza store with four tables at the front and a small counter with a few overcooked slices of pizza in a case on the counter. Jas grabbed hold of the counter as if he was about to tear it off when suddenly the boy Jose ran past Carol with a giggle and darted under the counter top just as Jas flipped open the top, revealing a hinged top like a Dutch door, only sideways.

"Jose you little shit!" shouted Jas as the boy disappeared into the kitchen at the back. They headed out the back of the pizza kitchen to a common corridor shared by all the shops along the strip mall where they entered a long corridor with a few old air conditioners on the back wall of shops rattling away. They came to the back of what appeared to be something between a computer store and TV repair shop.

"Steve, hey!" gestured Jas as the two men fist bumped, and shadow box a little,

"What's this?" Steve asked, "Not your type," he added on. "Ain't she a little skinny for you?" he said and chuckled.

"Carol here is going to help us with tracking down ex's." Steve looked at Jas completely ignorant for a second.

"Look…" said Jas, "I told Carol here if she helps us track down and set up a few exes' we can score enough to get her a doctor and fix up the bruise on her head. She was going to bait a few ex-husbands so we could recover the money they screwed their ex-wives over for and we could get our fee and get her to a clinic for a brain scan or something."

"The boy!" blurted out Carol, "Don't forget the boy."

"That's going to take a lot more money, you know that right?" Jas informed Carol.

"Sure, I know," said Carol, "but I'm not leaving him like this and besides my head does not feel that bad."

"What about your eye?" asked Jas.

"Yes, that could do with a look at," Carol replied as she walked to the front of the shop to browse the collection of old TVs and computers.

Steve grasped Jas by the shoulder, looking him square in the eyes and said, "Ok what's all this bullshit?"

Jas replied, "I will fill you in as we go, but she thinks we are some kind of detective agency tracking down ex-husbands and getting back money owed to their ex-wives, using some unconventional methods."

"And she's buying this?" asked Steve.

"For the moment it seems to be working. You're just flying by your ass on this one."

"Ah fuck off," said Jas. "She is also a mark."

Steve's eyes widen as if he was about to be hit by a bus, "What the fuck?" asked Steve.

"Complicated!" said Jas, "She lost her memory, and I've got to keep her close and do some job at the same time, so I made a cover story, and so far she seems to be taking to it."

"Thin... very fucking thin," said Steve.

"It's working," said Jas, "So just go with it."

"Hmm…" said Steve, "People really are so gullible and easy to scam."

"So long as all parts fit together well enough? Yes," said Jas.

Carol took comfort seeing the young boy busy spinning himself dizzy on a shop stool, she marveled at how the boy was quite untroubled and chuckled to herself as he most assuredly was putting on a show to garner her attention. She found a certain comfort in the boy's antics and his apparent detachment for all else other than her, as if somehow only both of them were the only things real, and she realized a sense of relief for the first time since waking up to this weird world and dream she found herself in at that point.

Carol looked at herself in the mirror on the shop wall as she started to wonder who she might actually be. A school teacher, perhaps? *No, can't be*, she thought *What the hell would a school teacher be doing here anyway? Kids? Do I have kids?*' She grabbed her firm and fit stomach, *Not likely with this tight tummy!* She felt her arms and thighs toned and firm, *Couldn't be a Mom.* She figured...*What mom ever has time to keep this fit?...Nice, though.* What about this story Jas had told her? Sort of fitted with a detective and she wondered if maybe that was what she was, some sort of detective?

SIX
Getting Down To Business

Jas beckoned Carol, "This way." He led her as they entered a small office at the back of the shop with a number of computers and work stations around the room on a table that ran along the wall for three sides of the room. Scattered between the work stations were a series of alarm clocks and a few racks with a few three ring binders for each work station.

"Sit here," as Jas commanded pulling back a swivel chair for Carol. "I'll show you what you do." Jas turned on the computer and some other devices on the desk, he logged into a folder filled with several other folders. Each labeled with a person's face, name, and profile.

"Here are a bunch of ex-husbands who had not only married their women for money but also cheated on their wives. We have been hired by the ex-wives to retrieve as much of their losses back from these scumbags. We don't get paid till we get whatever sum the ex-wives want to get back."

"Why don't they hire their own lawyer to do this rather than get us to do it?"

"Lawyers? You're kidding me? Lawyers are the biggest liars. Haven't you realized the word itself comes from the word LIARS? You dumb or what?"

"I just feel it'd be more appropriate to engage them is all."

"Here's what you gonna be doin."

Jas filled Carol in on her tasks one by one.

"And some of them will be a little tougher to deal with so you would need to work on them for about a month or so. Any questions?"

"Yes, I still don't understand what stories you want me to share with them."

Jas looked up with his eyes rolling and shaking his head, "Oh God! Why did you have to send us this fool?" and he continued, "Before you even contact them, you will read the notes written under their profile. Find out more about them. Then think of a strategy and how you want to get their attention. Remember what I told you right from the start... you are Carol, and you look like this." He flashed a picture of a tall, sexy, Asian model-like lady in her late 30s, in Carol's face.

"Why do I want to lie to him about what I really look like?"

"Look, woman, my patience is running low. You just hear me out, and get working on the first ex-husband. And check out your own profile and identity before you call them. God! You think you don't even know who you really are? It's all written in that folder. Your true identity and all. Ok? Ok? O–"

"K, I'll try. Stop behaving so impatiently with me, ok?" interrupted Carol.

As she referred to the contents of the folder, she began to think she had been hired as a private investigator and her department handled ex-wives who had been cheated by their spouses not only financially or due to extra marital affairs but also because the former had been victims of mental, verbal or physical abuse. These ex-wives engaged their service to get back at their ex-husbands and wanted to take things into their own hands because they had all lost everything during their legal proceedings against the men.

Rachel entered the room towards Jas' workstation and whispered to him, "I want you to let her observe how you deal with one of your catches before you let her work on hers. This bitch is too honest and emotional to be doing what we do."

Jas shouted across the room at Carol, "Hey, come over here." He used hand gestures to direct her to his work station.

Carol walked up to him and asked, "Now what?"

"I'm gonna call this man," Jas said as he pointed at a man's picture with a caption that read Michael, 56 years old, West Vancouver, Canada, on his Macbook screen, "Just listen and don't utter a single word, ok?" Jas set up his MorphVox before he made his call as Carol nodded and sat right behind him curiously listening and watching his every move. MorphVox was a free software used to disguise a person's voice. In this case, Jas used it to disguise himself to sound like a sexy woman.

"How are you, my love?" Jas sounded so head over heels as he spoke to the person at the other end.

"I miss you, baby," the man replied in a mushy tone, "How's your mom? Did the operation go well?"

"She's resting. My cousin's called to give me updates. I wish I could go see her. If not for my student loans–"

"How much is the flight ticket, baby?"

"I'm not too sure. I've never bothered to check anyway."

"Go check it out. I'll get it for you. I know what it's like to be so far away from home. Or would you rather I bought it online for you?"

"I think I can purchase it myself. It's really complicated, there are a couple of airports in the city where my mom lives. But are you sure you will get me the ticket?"

"Yes, positive. If I'm not so tied up with work, I wouldn't mind joining you so we could have our own rendezvous too."

"Oh honey, I don't think I'd be in the mood. All I want is to visit my mom and care for her."

"Sure, baby. Sorry, I've been so tactless. Go check out the ticket. Oh yeah, how much do you owe in student loans?"

"Too much. I don't want to talk about that right now."

"C'mon, baby. What's mine is yours. Just let me know. If I'm able to help, I will. Then you can finally apply for a visa and make a trip here, and we could finally be together soon."

"The last I remembered I owe about $95K in student loans. The damn interest keeps inflating."

"I can loan you half if you want. What do you think?"

"Let me think about that cos no one has ever helped me in my life and I feel so indebted to you, honey."

"No, baby. I just want you to get over with all this shit in your life, and we can be whole."

"Really? You serious about this?"

"Yeah, just pass me your account details and I'll get funds transferred."

"I'll text you details later. I need to get back to work. I love you."

"Gimme a kiss, baby."

Jas kissed through the phone speaker as if he were really kissing someone affectionately. Then hung up the phone.

Jas sent Michael a text with full details of a bank account belonging to a Janet E Crawford. Before Carol could ask who Janet was, Michael texted back to ask the same question. Jas lied that Janet was his roommate and added "I can't start a bank account here, hun. I've got a huge debt and bad credit. They won't let me get my own. In fact, I wouldn't want my own account either cos creditors will put a lien on whatever assets are in my name."

It didn't take long for Michael to reply, "My poor baby. Do you think we can trust Janet with so much money?"

"Yes, she can be trusted. She has helped me a lot all these years."

Alright, I'll get $20k transferred to the account by tomorrow. Use some for your trip back to Poland to visit your mom."

"I love you, hun. God is so kind to have blessed me with a guy like you. Thank you."

"I love you too baby. I want you here by Thanksgiving."

Carol tried to piece that story, yet confusion was written all over her as she was unable to understand what had exactly transpired.

Jas looked at her and told her he'd just made a total of $90k from Mike since he connected with him 3 months ago. He further explained that all these while Michael thought he got matched with Jasmine, a single, sexy, blond Polish American lady in her late 20s who was living and working in Marlton, New Jersey. Jasmine had been providing Mike with phone sex and sexting on a regular basis and because of her huge debts and her busy work schedule, had been unable to join him for another year. Michael, a 56-year-old divorcee, owned a construction business in British Columbia and had made a promise to Jasmine that he would want to make a trip to New Jersey by year end after he was done with his current projects. He e-met Jasmine on Skype twice before Jasmine claimed her wifi at home had been terminated due to some roadworks going on in her neighborhood. They'd been in contact via their cell phones on a daily basis.

Just as Jas was explaining the whole story to Carol, the alarm clock on his desk rang. "Time for another sucker!" This time, Jas didn't use any software, but just went through his phone directory and called a girl by the name of Tina.

"Hi, baby. How's your day so far?" Jas asked

"Miss you so much, Dennis."

"Me too, babe. I've had such a long day. It's almost midnight here, and I just got off work. So damn shack." Jas complained sounding exhausted....."No babe, I can't visit you just yet. I can't get off this project at the moment. They dumped me with yet another project. And you know the damn student loan I'm paying is driving me insane."

As Jas was conversing on the phone with Tina, Carol scrutinized his workstation and noticed notes tugged in each folder labeled with a name. There was one belonging to a Mike, Tina, Sasha, Josh, Robert, and he had downloaded quite a few interesting software and apps on his own Macbook Pro. Curious to know what exactly was going on, Carol looked around the room and noticed how the rest of the crew comprising about six to eight of them working. Everyone was dressed in expensive brands, some wearing gold bracelets, necklaces and high end watches. All of them looked below 30 and one or two of them as young as 19. As Jas continued to flirt in his conversation with Tina, Carol stood up and started walking to the other workstations to eavesdrop on the other colleagues' conversations. As she was approaching a tall, slim built guy, a familiar voice with a deep accent coming from her right caught her attention. She diverted to her right and walked towards that somewhat familiar voice. She stopped by the guy's workstation and looked at the guy straight into his eyes. She was sure she had heard that voice before and could hear her own inner soul trying to tell her something, but she wasn't able to decipher the. *That voice... I've heard that voice and accent before.... But from where could I have heard that from?* She asked herself, still feeling puzzled.

SEVEN
Who Are These People?

Carol walked up to that presumably familiar voice with high hopes that this person recognized her and would help solve her identity issue. *Please tell me you know something, anything. Perhaps we've met at a function or somewhere.* She thought to herself as she stood right behind the guy who was standing at approximately 6 feet tall. The minute he ended his phone conversation, Carol tapped on his shoulder and immediately he turned around.

"Hi," Carol reached out to him and asked, "Have we met somewhere before?"

The guy looked at her with his eyes wide open as though he had seen a ghost, before regaining his composure. "No, I don't believe so. Who are you? When did they hire an Asian chick?" The guy replied, trying hard to behave in a cool manner.

Before either could continue their conversation, Jas shouted out to her in a frustrated tone. "Hey, Carol. What the fuck you doing there? Come on back here!"

She found the guy's voice rather familiar, but not his face, and reminded herself, she had some work to do. She left the guy and walked back to Jas' workstation with a heavy heart.

"Did I tell you to roam around? Did I?" asked Jas, still sounding frustrated with her.

Carol shook her head and shed some tears as she made her way back to Jas' workstation.

"Why are you crying? What the hell's wrong with you?" Jas asked, once again getting impatient with her.

Carol decided to keep how she felt to herself and asked Jas what he wanted her to do next.

"Come follow me to Rachel's office and watch how I'm gonna prepare my Skype meeting with Tina. She wants to Skype me today." Jas went to the YouTube channel of a person by the name of Jeffrey and downloaded one of his 15 minute videos. He paused the video and pointed his webcam at Jeffrey's video then conducted a dry run to test the Skype call. He Skype his colleague who happened to sit at the workstation across from him and the minute his colleague accepted the Skype call, Jas played the muted YouTube video. Jas started talking over Skype and asked his colleague if the Skype reception looked authentic enough.

"All's good, Jas!" shouted the same colleague whom Carol approached from across the room with his thumbs up.

He sent Tina a text to ask if she's ready to Skype and she sent him a positive reply almost immediately.

Carol watched how Jas conducted his voice over with Tina on Skype. She could hear Tina repeatedly asking why their Skype reception seemed a little jerky and Jas complained about the poor WIFI connection he was experiencing, giving the excuse that it was possibly caused by some road work in front of his apartment. Carol studied the YouTube video carefully and noticed Jeffrey sitting in a hotel room throughout the conversation and Jas, known to Tina as Dennis, had made Tina think he was staying in a company apartment and that he was conducting the Skype conversation with her from his room. As the YouTube video approached an end, Jas immediately disconnected from his Skype conversation with Tina. He texted Tina to inform her his laptop was low on battery and apologized for not kissing her goodnight then told her he needed to go to bed as it was getting very late.

Carol told Jas she finally grasped what she was supposed to do and excused herself. She returned to her own workstation and searched for Jeffrey's YouTube channel to find out more about him. "This Jeffrey guy might know what's happening here. That face... I must have seen that face somewhere," She mumbled to herself confidently.

After much scrutinizing, she discovered Jeffrey was an innocent party who was a famous spiritual marketer in Southern California. She started piecing everything together and realized Jas was pretending to be Dennis and had been using Jeffrey's pictures and videos to catfish Tina. 'But why is Tina a target? What did she do to become his target?' She was still as puzzled as ever, but she was confident that she was getting another step closer to discovering who she really was.

EIGHT
Carol, The Storyteller

After a few days watching how Jas convinced his 'better half' with his stories and managed to get what he wanted, Carol started her quest as a storyteller. At the back of her mind, she could hear Jas' exact words, "Get them hooked and you'll get what you want cos they'll come back for more."

She searched for a new profile in the folder of her Macbook and was intrigued by a woman named Cara, a 30-year-old single, blond beauty, civil engineer, who was cheated by her boyfriend 3 years ago and had never gotten involved in a relationship again. She had a couple of responsibilities to manage, from a mortgage to paying bills to care for her sick, widowed mother back in Prague. Before she used the images of a beautiful, blond European lady to match Cara's profile, she uploaded her photos on Tineye just to be sure her image had not been used elsewhere, and her true identity was not disclosed all over cyberspace. "Nope, can't use this one," she mumbled and sighed to herself, "red alert all over. One of these guys has used images of her before." Carol started searching for another image with the same criteria and discovered a profile of a beautiful lady from the U.S. and went through the same process. This time, nothing was flagged. She searched YouTube channels for someone who resembled this lady to build the database, just in case there was a request to Skype or Facetime her. She got very excited when she discovered the woman was a successful business owner from Utah who happened to have her own YouTube channel and was moderately active on social media.

She found this girl on Facebook and noticed that her friends list, as well as photo albums, were not secured so Carol downloaded as many photos possible and saved them in a folder. She used this lady's photos and created a new profile with a new name. Carol's new identity was now Hannah as she started her conquest to catfish new victims. She installed a location faker app on her phone and for some reason, her intuition got her to point towards Vancouver, BC. She settled for a location downtown Vancouver and started installing several online dating apps on the phone. On Tinder, Match.com, and several other dating apps, including all platforms which disclosed the distance a person was from the one the latter matched with in order for her to appear as though she was in Vancouver, BC. She started creating Hannah's profile, uploaded photos of the businesswoman from Utah and "Voila, Hannah is now supposedly in Vancouver, BC." She said to herself as though she had achieved a huge breakthrough.

She reminded herself to think a step ahead of questions her victim might ask. 'How do I masquerade myself and falsify my actual location?' She asked herself as she scanned through the manual that explained everything.

"Download Magic Jack to spoof a phone number so my number will seem like it's from Vancouver, B.C., on their caller ID." She read out loud to herself from the instruction manual. *Wow! Whoever invented these technologies sure make our job easy.* She gradually gained the trust of the perpetrators producing very effective results. Her storytelling efforts paid off as she managed to build a strong rapport with her victims and she eventually earned the title of Robin Hood winning the admiration of her co workerscoworkers. Her popularity increased as she managed to reap in over US $200k in 8 weeks through 3 very successful men from Canada.

NINE
Memory Sting

Carol had begun to adjust to life in the group and was now well versed at camouflaging herself and what she was feeling. Still unaware that she had lost her memory and that her true identity was Jamie Tan. Syndicate was obviously aware of, hoping she would never regain her memory because she had made them so much money since joining the organization. She seemed like a natural either because she had previously been a victim or because she was just incredibly smart and crafty.

As she continued with her new line of work and kept making progress, Rachel had now started taking her more seriously. Even Jas could not help but admire her because she just seemed fearless and unstoppable, and while she was able to get across to everyone in the Syndicate including the kids that were there, there was one particular individual who somehow was not moved by all she had accomplished either out of jealousy or pure dislike - no one could really tell. This particular individual had been watching her from his desk since the day Carol had successfully conned her first victim. He would clench his fist feeling bitter with anger whenever he noticed Carol had successfully scammed a new victim of their life savings and received praise from one of the Syndicate members. Douglas was average sized, in his mid-thirties, and was of Nigerian descent. He was recruited by the Syndicate after his poverty stricken parents sold him to Rachel's dad as a child where he started as a child labourer in one of Rachel's family plantations. Rachel's dad took notice that Douglas always went the extra mile, performing whatever labour was assigned to him and he decided to place him under the guidance of his then right hand man, Indra. Indra was one of the few people who was interested in exploring the use of computers and technology in the early days of the Syndicate.

All these while, Carol had tried to extend a hand of friendship to him, but he just declined and brushed her off repeatedly. One day at lunch, while everyone was in a jovial mood and Carol was having her lunch while the children played around, Douglas appeared out of nowhere telling the kids to play somewhere else so he could talk to her. Though the children expressed their displeasure, they had no choice but to go. Carol, however, was pleasantly surprised, seeing a ray of hope and thinking she had finally won Douglas over to her side.

The minute he sunk into his chair, his facial expression changed from being completely nonchalant to a look of disgust. He started hurling vulgarities at her and pointed his finger right in her face "...and you bitch, you took everything away from me, yet you walk around like you're some kind of flavour of the month! Like you're better than the rest of us! Well, newsflash, girl, you're nothing, and no matter what you do, you will never be better than me." His attitude and remark came as a shocker to her, leaving her dumbfounded as she watched him stand, kick his chair to the side and walk away. She was speechless and felt like crying that instant because never in her life had she been insulted or regarded as a threat, and suddenly she realized she was in a world where people she surrounded herself with seem threatened by her existence.

When word got out about what Douglas did, many of the members were disappointed except for Rachel and Jas, who were largely unmoved because they knew the kind of person he was, but they could not eliminate him since he was exceptionally useful to the organization. Apart from being one of their best agents, before Carol anyway, he also helped with any technical issues and had ties to other organizations that protected the interests of Rachel and the Syndicate. This gave him immunity. He could pretty much do whatever he wanted. Besides, he was an introvert that rarely interacted with anyone, which made it difficult for people to predict his motives. Whatever move he made, they had no choice but to go with it and accept it.

Rachel ordered Carol to her office and apologized to her, reasoning that Douglas was just Douglas, and she should keep doing her thing and try to ignore his existence. She shrugged off the whole situation and continued with her activities for the group. After the previous assignment in which she ripped off a 30-year-old civil engineer, she was given a break by Rachel, and while she had to stay within the boundaries where the Syndicate was based, she had enough 'me-time' and a lot of free time on her hands to do whatever she liked.

After her early morning work-out which she now had more time for, she had breakfast, surfed the internet and then took a walk later in the evening. Sometimes, she read books. Other times, she just played with the kids, read books to them or played games with them. Strangely enough, the best parts of her time off were usually time spent with the children. She could just imagine herself being a mother someday. She imagined being married with a lovely husband and two beautiful kids staying in the suburbs with all the peace and tranquillity she could ever wish for. *Such an ideal level of bliss and fantasy*, she thought to herself before being brought out of her reverie by one of the kids who tripped and twisted his ankle.

He was taken to the clinic meant for the organization and Carol stayed up with him all night without blinking her eyes to comfort the boy. She helped entertain him and soothed his ankle till he fell asleep.

In the morning, she left the hospital to go to her room and steal some sleep. She began to dream, there were kids running around the park, calling "Mama, Mama, it's your turn." She woke up sweating profusely that strange realization that the fantasy scene she'd imagined the day before was now showing up in her dreams. She went to the bathroom and splashed some water onto her face and cleaned herself up a bit before she headed back to the clinic to check on the boy.

Just as she was about to step through the clinic door, Carol slipped on a puddle of liquid and fell, banging the back of her head roughly on the ground. She was unconscious once again. She was rushed and treated at the clinic immediately. After being unconscious for 2 days, she found herself in a dream similar to the one she'd had a few days earlier. This time, there were two Asian kids who looked alike and resembled her. She could also hear a familiar voice which seemed to be calling out for her, "Jamie, come on, let's go, the kids are waiting for you," but she just stood wondering who Jamie was. Eventually, she was woken by a few slaps on her cheek, and as she opened up eyes, she looked up to see the doctor, Rachel and some of the kids together with Jas smiling at her. For some reason, she found it difficult to smile back, but she tried waving her hands to them. The doctor then explained to them that she could be feeling exhausted and required more rest.

A few days later, Carol was back on her feet and feeling more like her old self, smiling and playing with people. The doctor still checked up on her regularly to ascertain her state of health and after about a week, then he declared her 100% fit. Since there was no time to waste, Rachel recalled her for another assignment and demanded that she reported for duty the following day.

TEN
Surprise! Surprise!!

Downtown Prague, a young man of about 28 years old was talking on the phone to another man from his office in a low rise building. That young man was Bertrand, the head of operations for Syndicate covering all of Europe with their headquarters in the Czech Republic.

"How is it going over there, my man?" Bertrand asked his counterpart.

"It's going fine man, business is good, and more people just keep falling in line; guess people are suckers for love and sympathy," the man on the other end of the line replied.

"Well, it's the way of the world, and we are just great at capitalizing the situation."

The man smiled and laughed, "Exactly, so have you heard anything from Rachel about the meeting next month?"

"Nothing new. Same time, date and venue. Guess we shall see, but till then, let's just keep the flag flying."

Bertrand dropped the phone and rubbed his mustache, thinking of the current victim, he was dealing with, a 55-year-old British man from Germany known as Gordon. The man was fortunate enough to inherit family riches and had turned it into a fortune. He'd only recently divorced and was desperately in need of someone to love and genuinely care for him. He was surfing the internet one day and decided to check out Tinder, Plenty of Fish, and several other online dating platforms which a friend of his had earlier introduced to him. After about a week of clicking on the profiles of several ladies and sending messages with no reply, he finally got a message from a certain Sandra, who was an American residing in the United Kingdom. He was so excited that he almost jumped up in ecstasy. From then on, they started talking and began to get to know each other better.

Sandra was a successful businesswoman who had a large, profitable store where she sold different kinds of high end fashion items. Gradually their relationship blossomed even without meeting each other in person, but it was all one-sided in terms of the feelings as Sandra was none other than Bertrand and the pictures he had used belonged to a lady working for him, who was oblivious about what was going on at the back end of the office. She was simply told her pictures were needed to help the company generate more customers and sales to which she gladly obliged without even thinking about any possible consequences that might emerge.

Now Bertrand knew that he was treading on thin ice ever since he sent a message to the man and discovered that he was based in Germany.

Their organization had never experienced a successful stint in Germany because of the high level of security from authorities fighting against money laundering and other fraudulent activities. He was confident the money he was about to extort from Gordon would outweigh all the risks involved. As he was deep in his scheming thoughts, there came a knock on his door. It was Samantha, the girl whose pictures had been used for profiles created by Bertrand on online dating portals - she entered to inform him of someone interested in seeking marriage counselling. Syndicate had created a marriage counselling service to front their venture in the Czech Republic to cover up their illegal activities since they penetrated Europe.

Bertrand ushered him in and after about an hour, he came out smiling because he seemed to have been provided with the solution. With that Bertrand went out to grab a quick lunch and relaxed before going back to the office to tie up loose ends.

Three weeks passed, Bertrand, impersonated Sandra and was about to make his move on Gordon. 'She' shared with him about how 'her' business had not been moving as expected and that she needed a loan of around a million Euros to stock up her inventory that would help revive the business. The man was filled with sympathy for her and went on to probe if she was able to obtain a loan from the bank in her country of residence. She answered that banks would always be looking over her shoulder, but with him, she would be able to pay back on a regular instalment yet had the flexibility of operating her business in the most effective manner. Gordon agreed, then added that he was not able to wire the money, but preferred to pass her the funds in person. He went on to further elaborate that it would also be a great opportunity for them to actually meet for the first time. Bertrand was silent for a while, and then he smiled and agreed, assuring Gordon "No problem."

About an hour later, Bertrand was deep in thoughts about how was he going to meet Gordon face-to face; while they have pulled it off before, it was never in Germany, but in Czech which was where their European Headquarters was located thus making it easier then. Furthermore, they had no branch or agency in Germany, which meant no backup or secured property whatsoever. He decided he was going to go solo on this to prove to Syndicate he was fit for his post. He determined that he was going to use Samantha, the lady working for him, to fulfil the job. After all, it was her pictures he had been using to pose as Sandra. He decided to send her an email about the plan and with that he went to bed confidently, looking forward for the big day to arrive.

The next day, Samantha met up with her boss at the airport, and they travelled down to Frankfurt in Germany. On arrival, Bertrand called Gordon and instructed Samantha to inform him they had arrived. She did as instructed by her boss but was surprised when Gordon addressed her as Sandra. She asked for the place to meet and was told to head to Commerzbank located in the heart of Frankfurt, which for a time had been involved in money laundering activities particularly in connection with the Middle East. This was where he would withdraw the money which he had planned on loaning to her. Bertrand had told her that the money was payment for a job earlier carried out for the man to which Samantha shrugged and simply followed instructions.

Damn, why must it be with Commerzbank again? Bertrand thought to himself as he started to have mixed feelings about the bank transfer. He had failed once before trying to get the funds through that same bank in Germany. He wasn't really sure what to expect this time

While Samantha went for the 'rendezvous', Bertrand was in the hotel feeling anxious while at the same time thinking of how he was going to show off to other members at the meeting that he had single-handedly pulled off one of the greatest jobs in Syndicate's history.

Samantha finally got to meet Gordon. They hugged each other, smiling as they sat and started talking,

"Hi Samantha, how was your trip darling?"

"It was fine, Graham and I hope you have been well."

"I have definitely been well, except for the thief who wants to rob me of my hard-earned money. You've done a terrific job so far. Very impressive."

"His time is up anyway and hopefully. He will lead us to the rest of his cohorts."

"Well, let's get going then, shall we?"

She went back to the hotel with a briefcase that Graham had passed her. Graham and a few other men followed her closely while taking care to blend in with the crowd. In the elevator, Graham handed Samantha a weapon to conceal, and as the elevator door was about to open, he wished her luck. Before she could knock on Bertrand's room door, he opened it, smiling and beaming at her with excitement, "Oh, welcome darling"- a gentle and caring tone he had never used on her before because he always felt she was too sheepish and dull.

"Thank you," she replied.

"I see Gordon fell for our ploy. I must say I am impressed by you. Let's check our loot in the briefcase."

She handed over the briefcase to him, only to meet the shocker of his life because it was empty, as he turned to face her in rage and was about to beat the life out of her before calming down to demand to know what had transpired, he was met with a strong kick in the face that sent him sprawling to the other end of the room. Before he could gather himself, the victim, Gordon, with the rest of his men broke their way in and Bertrand more shocked than before was arrested and whisked away.

Unknown to Bertrand all the while, he had been suspected of money laundering and the German authorities had devised a plan to plant Inspector Agneta Otto from the Flensburg police district in Germany to pose as Samantha to work for Bertrand.   For the past 3 months, Agneta had been trying to get as much evidence as possible through Bertrand's organization, but the Syndicate had been managed so well by Bertrand she wasn't able to find enough leads on the case. This time, their investigation unit hoped to unfold as much of as possible with Bertrand in custody. They started their search for the mastermind since the Flensburg unit was left with no other choice but to release Malley due to the lack of evidence to prosecute him.

ELEVEN
A Mix In The Game

Back in North Carolina was a group of people seated in a large boardroom dressed mostly in Armanis, JPGs, and Pradas, ready to discuss the latest activities of their individual organization. Observing those in attendance gave the impression that the meeting was to discuss how to make positive contributions to human existence or to improve the lives of others. On the contrary, they were nothing more than a bunch of criminals gathering to discuss strategies to increase profits carrying out various forms of underground activities.

The group was none other than Syndicate, who was expert at scamming people and robbing them of their money, mostly in the name of love and business ventures. Seated at the head of the table was Rachel Domino, who was the leader of Syndicate, an organization she inherited from her dead father, Nicolas Domino. Seated to her right was Jas, a loyal and astute follower who was also her right hand man and to her left was Douglas, a man who was unassuming and mysterious. Carol was also given a seat at the table due to her meteoric rise since being forcefully inducted into Syndicate. The meeting commenced with each individual representative from each continent delivering their reports, starting from Asia with emphasis on Kuala Lumpur, Malaysia. Each division started with the amount of profits they had made if the number of victims seemed to have increased over the past few months and with how flawlessly their branches had performed when it came to delivering their percentage to the headquarters. Overall, the reports seemed impressive given it was their quarterly meeting, Rachel was pleased, but she felt something still seemed amiss. In fact, someone was missing from this important meeting.

From hacking bank accounts and social media platforms to extorting money from unsuspecting victims. They never ran out of creativity when performing new criminal activities, after all, 75% of criminal acts are initiated with the use of Information Technology. With the popularity of using WIFI to connect the world as it was becoming more and more seamless, there seemed to be better ways to scam the world.

"I've heard from a source that terrorists will gradually phase out suicide bombers to replace their invasions with the use of WIFI." Rachel told the group.

"Any idea how?" One of the members asked.

"Not certain, but they are planning on using google's idea of self-driven automobiles as a remotely guided weapon to launch more attacks. I don't really have the full picture but that's what I've heard from a reliable source. That's also one reason why they have requested that our organization help increase funding."

Just then, Carol's phone beeped, and everyone diverted their attention to her. It was against the rule to bring any phones or electronic device to the meeting. All members were expected to deposit their phones outside the boardroom and provisions had been made for that to be done. Carol hadn't done so because she felt she was just there as an observer. Earlier that morning, Jas had told her, "You are only invited to this meeting to observe how things are done and it's no big deal if you were to leave anytime during the meeting, but just to show you we are beginning to see the value in your contributions and think you are a potential asset, I am inviting you to join us. Get it?"

She immediately apologized, explaining that the call was work related from a potential victim. Just as she was about to go and start rambling on her story about the caller, up came Rachel's hand to wave her off, "Don't interrupt our meeting, woman, we don't want to hear it," and though Jas was not happy with Carol, he had to hold his peace. Carol immediately shut her mouth, turned off her phone and remained seated.

Eventually, Carol was told to leave them, complying almost immediately. Before Carol could get to the threshold, though, she heard Rachel's voice laced with concern.

"Where in the world is Bertrand? He told me he was going to be here to give his report about our operations in Europe as well as enlighten us on how we are going to break into Germany."

Just then a young man ran into the room and brought Rachel's phone saying she had an emergency call. With that, she grabbed her phone from him to find out what the emergency was. She was informed of Bertrand's arrest, which puzzled her because he was a smart guy. She sighed, cursing under her breath as her brain shot into overdrive.

The meeting was brought to an abrupt end. Rachel had a lot of respect for Bertrand because of his brains and shrewdness in seemingly impossible situations. She couldn't mention how she felt about him because he had a number of detractors and most of them were present at that meeting, so asking for their help was not an option. She reassured herself that Bertrand would get his name cleared by the cops, although immediately after that, she had a stinging feeling that this was something different, and she was going to need all the help she could get.

Meanwhile, Carol was back in her room, and for the fun of it, she thought to herself, *I want to know who will I attract just by using my own profile for once.* So this time instead of using someone else's photo and impersonating them under another fictitious name, she created a new profile on Tinder for herself. She decided to take a snapshot of herself, uploaded it to her own profile and even use her own name, Carol. *And this time, I shall just swipe all potential male profiles to the right just for the fun of it!* She thought to herself. Within minutes, she got matched with 3 male prospects. She started chatting with them, but one of them caught her attention. He happened to be a handsome 6 foot 2, claiming to be a successful architect from British Columbia, Canada. His name was Rob, he claimed his girlfriend had just died in an accident, and he had finally decided to move on with his life and start dating again. He wanted to give Tinder a shot and was pleasantly surprised to have matched with Carol. He posted images of all the buildings he and his team had developed and shared information with Carol about his life. He told her she reminded him of his girlfriend, Jamie. As they kept chatting, Carol could feel a strong connection between them. She was also curious about his girlfriend, that name seemed to ring a bell. *I seem to know what Jamie is like, but for some reason, that name sends chills down my spine. Who is Jamie?* Carol wanted to know what Jamie was like and asked Rob to tell her more about her.

"You look like Jamie, except that you've got a scar on your forehead," he explained to her. *"Please tell me more about yourself, Carol,"* he continued.

"Frankly, Rob. I have no idea who I really am," Carol admitted to him. For some reason, she had a good feeling about Rob and felt as though she had known him forever. *"I woke up one day, surrounded by my colleagues, and for some reason, the only thing I could remember was my own name. I have no idea who I'm related to nor do I even have a family. I work for a matchmaking agency and have been with them ever since."*

"Is there a possibility you are not who you think you are, Carol?" Rob messaged back.

Carol read that sentence repeatedly and decided to call it a day as she got more and more confused about herself. *"Let's chat tomorrow, Rob. I need to go now, BBFN,"* she replied, logging out of Tinder.

Back in B.C., David was feeling a little disturbed about his encounter with Carol. He wanted to ask her more questions, but she had already logged out of her account. He kept looking at Carol's picture and profile and something in him raised suspicion that Carol might be Jamie. *But what the heck is she doing in North Carolina?* He thought to himself. *Should I disclose my true identity to her? What if her life's in danger? Should I file a police report? Fuck, our law enforcement here's a bunch of morons. Maybe I should head to North Carolina myself? Maybe...* David started forming a never ending string of questions as he went back to read the chat messages between Carol and himself.

All these while, David had been searching everywhere for Jamie, and when news from the Maryland authorities confirmed that Jamie's whereabouts could not be traced, he filed a report of a missing person over there and in B.C. After months of fruitless searching, he reached the point of desperation that he decided to work against his principles and join Tinder. David had always been against and very weary of all kinds of online dating platforms, but this time, he even got his profile registered online, under the name of Rob White. For months now, he had been frantically searching for Jamie to no avail, yet he refused to give in to the thought that she was gone forever. All his vacation time off was spent riding on his Harley travelling to various states in the U.S. in search of his beloved friend.

He already knew about romance scams as well as various social media sites that were used to perpetrate their evil work, which was why he registered on various online dating portals. Finally, he got matched with Carol on Tinder and immediately received a message from her. He wasn't sure if his new match on Tinder was a fraud and had only intended to play along with the hope of getting some leads, but during their conversation that very day, Carol slipped up, and he managed to get clues from her that she was based in North Carolina. He didn't want to get his hopes high as he still wasn't sure who Carol was. Days passed, and he started getting more and more comfortable with Carol as they kept communicating with each other. He had a strong feeling Carol was indeed Jamie, yet he wanted to be very cautious with her till he was able to prove her true identity. He decided to track her down as he started his research on various types of software he could use to find the perpetrators. He cautioned himself that the picture featured under Carol's profile might have been catfished and kept reminding himself to stay on guard as he dealt with Carol. He remained patient and stealthy about it and decided to make a trip to North Carolina on his motorcycle.

TWELVE
A Twist of Fate

David kept in touch with Carol throughout his journey to North Carolina. He would check his messages whenever he stopped to fill up the gas tank, or whenever he took his breaks. He was now beginning to piece things together, but he was still confused as to who Carol was. "How the hell did she end up as Carol? Who's Carol?" Each time he attempted to shrug the thought off, there was the feeling that Carol was Jamie, and so he kept conversing with her and finally he asked her one day, "*Do you have any children, Carol? I would want to have my own kids someday, and I'd love to name them Russell and Raymond if I ever had twin boys*." Those names seemed to jolt her memory, and while she already had the feeling that her real name was not Carol ever since she banged her head after slipping on that clinic floor, she still could not figure out what her real name was, until now.

"*Those names—*" The names seemed to trigger Carol as she typed in the chat box to Rob. "*Those names seem very familiar to me. How did I get here?*" Carol continued.

David's heart sank when he read that last sentence from Carol. Something had struck his thoughts as he was sure Carol was Jamie, that perhaps she was forced into committing some form of underground crime and needed some help. He decided to lay it all out for her. "*Sweet, does the name David Smith ring a bell? I am quite familiar with the scamming process you are involved in, and I understand you're a victim. I am willing to help you with certain resources and skill set at my disposal. I just need you to cooperate by telling me the truth so that we can come up with a definite solution.*"

Carol paused and thought about everything that Rob had mentioned. It seemed as though a jolt of light had passed through her spine. When David saw no response, he sent her another message "*Are you there sweet?*" to which she replied "*Yes.*" Being addressed as 'sweet' sounded so familiar because the only person who used to call Jamie by the pet name, "Sweet," was David.

Realizing her true identity was Jamie, though the recollection of her past still remained pretty vague, she gradually opened up and explained all she had gone through and what she had been doing for the Syndicate. David was gushing with hope. He was quite certain he had been communicating with Jamie on Tinder this whole while. He had mixed feelings and wasn't sure if he had done the right thing disclosing his true identity to her at that moment and neither was he sure what to do next. He looked at the GPS on the dashboard of his motorcycle and realized he was only in Des Moines, Iowa, another one thousand miles away from North Carolina. He became desperate to save Jamie there and then.

Meanwhile, Carol had turned off her phone as she was feeling very confused after reading Rob's messages. Certain things Rob had mentioned seemed a little perplexing to her. She looked at her own reflection in the mirror feeling so frustrated with herself as the thought of those names Jamie, Russell, and Raymond seemed so familiar to her, yet she wasn't able to associate them with anyone she could recollect. Her instincts told her not to break ties with Rob not to con the guy of his savings, but to try to probe more into him before she did anything else. She decided to defy Syndicate's rules and started deleting all messages she encountered with Rob after reading them.

That night Carol tried to calm herself as she lay in bed exhausted from the events she had encountered. She struggled to stay awake trying to connect whatever information Rob had shared with her that day. Before she could piece the story any further, she succumbed to exhaustion and fell deeply asleep. Her unconscious mind wandered off, as she started to experience flashbacks from her past.

******

THIRTEEN
FLASHBACK

March 5th, 2015, 7.00am PST

Jamie got notified of a new match on Tinder. She checked her app and noticed she had been matched with a guy by the name of Daniel. Jamie checked the distance they were apart from each other and realized it was approximately 24km. Daniel immediately initiated sending her text messages.

Daniel: *Hey, how are you?*

Jamie: *I am good. Thank you.*

Daniel: *I am so happy we got matched. My name's Daniel Slovák.*

Jamie: *Pleased to meet you. I'm Jamie.*

Daniel: *So what are you up to today?*

Jamie: *Usual stuff.*

Daniel: *Just curious, where were you originally from?*

Jamie: *That's for you to guess. Lunch on me if you can guess it right. Otherwise, dinner's on you.*

Daniel: *Deal!*

Jamie: *So make a guess while I get ready for work. I can only give you one clue. I am neither a Korean or Japanese.*

Daniel: *Singapore Chinese?*

"Damn! How in the world did he get the answer correct at his first try?" Jamie wondered aloud as she braced her weight against the bed to slip on her other heel.

Jamie decided to text back, *"What made you think so?"*

Daniel: *I just got back from Singapore 2 months ago. I looked at your photos and your profile, you don't seem like a typical Asian. So do I take it that lunch is on you?*

Jamie: *Alright. Let's do it some other time. Heading to work now. BBFN*

Daniel: *Text me when you are available ok?*

Jamie didn't bother to respond and logged out of Tinder for the day.

Daniel started a string of text messages as both of them got to know each other better.

They began conversing online via Tinder for the next 2 days. Daniel told Jamie he was leaving for Maryland as he was only in Vancouver on business. He was done with his meetings with a Canadian company which was entering into a joint venture with his company. He was supposed to head back to Maryland and settle all the administrative work. He gave Jamie his contact number and told her he was going to remove the Tinder app as he wasn't a fan of apps and online dating. Besides, he felt he had found his match and didn't think he wanted to stay on with Tinder as he had been receiving other messages from women who seemed desperate for hook ups. Jamie, on the other hand, made it clear to Daniel that she wasn't into any long distance relationship and would prefer to just remain friends with him if he was ok with her decision. Daniel assured her she didn't need to worry about that because he was actually returning to Canada once his work permit was approved. Given his occupation and the fact that the Canadian company was willing to sponsor his company's application, he was very confident he would be returning to Vancouver within the next two to three months. Jamie told him to just let nature take its course. If it was meant to be, it would.

FOURTEEN
An Element of Love

March 5th, 8:00pm PST

Daniel sent a text to Jamie claiming he was about to board his flight to return to Maryland. He told her he should be back in Vancouver soon and wanted to meet her by then if she was still available. Meanwhile, he hoped to get to know her even better despite the distance between them.

Jamie just smiled to herself and sent him a message wishing him a safe journey home. She started to think to herself, "Hmm, let's see how long he would last the minute he knows about my boys!"

March 6th, 7:00am PST

Daniel texted Jamie to inform her he had arrived in Maryland. Then sent her a picture he had taken with his colleague. He told her he had a good feeling about her and wanted to initiate a Skype conversation with her that evening.

8:00pm PST

They met face to face on Skype for the first time that night. He asked Jamie if she had Skyped with anyone else she met online before.

She kept complaining that the Skype video with him seemed laggy, and though she managed to see him, the video kept freezing while he was talking. She could hear him clearly, but the entire session was visually jerky. He explained that the apartment his company put him up in had poor internet connection and always found it challenging Skyping from the apartment. He added that sometimes his son got frustrated Skyping with him as well. Jamie explained that it was her second time connecting with someone she met through an online dating site, but she added that she discovered the first one was a potential scammer and dropped him immediately. Daniel convinced her that Skype was the real sure way to talk when people weren't able to meet each other face to face. He went on to tell her that even businesses held legitimate conferences via Skype, and he was so glad they were able to Skype.

During the Skype session, Daniel talked about his previous marriage to a socialite in Prague and that he had lived there for 12 years while they were married. As she was from a wealthy family, her dad controlled him and after 12 years of marriage, he finally asked for a divorce and gave full custody of his son, Dejan, to his ex-wife. He claimed his son was his life, though, he would never have to worry about the boy's future as the latter was already secured with a good trust fund from his ex-wife's family. His nasty divorce left him half a share of his matrimonial home which his powerful father-in-law managed to under value so he wasn't able to obtain a fair market value from it when they divided their matrimonial assets. He only managed to receive half a million Euros from the deal. He used part of it to pay off his parents' mortgage and saved the rest. He hoped to settle in a new country and invest it in a home of his own or in a business venture. Daniel went on to talk about his immediate family. His mother was Serbian, and his dad was from the Czech Republic, and they were both living in Belgrade. He went on to add that his dad had been suffering from respiratory problems and dementia and had been living in a hospice. His mother was pretty much the only next of kin left, and she was living alone at home. He had lost his sister, Berta, back in 1991 in a car accident. Jamie, with her soft spot for the elderly, felt so sad for Daniel's parents who had to experience losing their child years ago and were now living alone in Belgrade. He told Jamie he had told his mother all about her, and she had asked for Jamie's photos because she was excited to know what Jamie looked like. Daniel gave Jamie his email address and asked her to email him a couple of her photos and some taken with her kids so he could send them to his mom.

Jamie still couldn't believe that someone would actually fall for her considering she had 'extra baggage.'

Daniel cautioned her never to label her kids as 'extra baggage' and expressed the following to her:

> "My Pearl, nothing under this planet is new. It is you I want to get to know better, I don't care about whatever situation you're in. I am beginning to feel good about you. The kids are wonderful and I think everyone should see them that way. They should be celebrated because they are here on Earth. No one was born a mistake. If you really want and love someone, you must accept everything about them. Otherwise, you don't love them enough. You have my heart and love, and I promise with everything I am to stand by you, love you, protect you, care for you, the kids and be loyal to you. Most of all, I want to spend our later years together telling stories about our love."

They hit it off from then as Daniel was just the type of man Jamie had always dreamed of, business minded, 6 ft. 1 tall, handsome and an articulate gentleman. He had gorgeous deep blue eyes and well-groomed beard that resembled Adam Levine. He seemed like someone caring, ambitious and intelligent with a solid career, and most importantly, someone who promised to love her children as his own. He started to gain her trust over the next few days, addressing Jamie by the nickname, Pearl.

FIFTEEN
New Developments

March 7th, 9:00am PST

Jonathan and Jamie were having breakfast in the office pantry. "How's Tinder so far? Met any interesting people yet?" He asked in a flirtatious yet curious manner.

Jamie started telling him about Daniel and that she knew she was slowly falling for him. She showed Jonathan some of his photos while another colleague, Nicole, walked in. Nicole interceded and saw the pictures and interrupted to ask Jamie, "Wow, where did you find that gorgeous hunk?" Jonathan related the story to Nicole about how Jamie was introduced to Tinder as they left the pantry to start their shift.

March 9th, 7:00pm PST

Daniel sent Jamie a text

> *"Hey, Pearl. I just submitted my bid for a Texas contract. Please pray that I will get this job. It will be the turning point of my career as I get to place what I have designed to reality. I have taken years to work on this idea, and I hope this company will give me the contract."*

Jamie replied:

> *"Sure, I'll pray for you. I have no idea what your job is. Is it the same thing as the one you were supposed to work on in BC?"*

Daniel called Jamie to answer her text question:
"Pearl, I prefer to hear your voice then to text you back.
No, Pearl. The one in BC is with the American firm I am attached to. They are the ones who are applying the work permit for me. While I am waiting for the work permit, the company allows me to take on other jobs because I am only employed by them as a contractual staff. So while waiting for that work permit, I would rather try to do other jobs to earn more for myself and my parents.
My Pearl... I am beginning to love you more and more as the day goes by."

"I still have no idea what your job entails, but I'll pray that you will get it," Jamie replied feeling so touched by his gestures.

43

SIXTEEN
Cock & Bull

March 11th, 5.54am PST

Jamie received a friend request on Facebook from Daniel, but before she accepted it, she went through his profile. She noticed his friends' list was secured and kept private. She accepted his friend request and Daniel immediately sent a message wishing her a happy birthday. She started receiving text messages from David and several other friends in Asia. She replied to all the text and Facebook greetings one at the time and finally to Daniel.

"Thank you. You need to be here celebrating my next birthday with me ok? I will always be with you on yours. Another day closer for us to be together, my dear."

She scanned through his photos on Facebook and noticed he had been all over Europe and parts of Asia, and there were photos taken with other friends.

As she checked through the events recorded in his Facebook account, she received a following text from him:
"Expecting results of bid tomorrow. Fingers crossed... Lotto results also lol... Your birthday is gonna be a great day :) kiss."

"Thank you. You bought lottery tickets too? I've prayed for you. Have faith. You will win the bid."

"Yes, trying the Powerball for the first time. Will send you a snapshot of the lottery ticket soon. Alright my Pearl, Love you..."

Jamie received a snapshot of the Powerball tickets and texted back a thank you.

Just as she smiled to herself, she received another text message with a love song attached.

Jamie played the song and tears started rolling down her cheeks. She had never felt so overwhelmed with emotions nor had she felt so loved before.

"Thank you. You should just focus on your business and not worry about our relationship because we need to meet first. Talk to you later. By the way, I stopped going on Tinder since Friday. Today I had another match. I have unmatched the person cos I think I may have already found my soul mate and have been Tenderized."

5:00pm PST

Jamie returned home from work, and her twins led her excitedly to the kitchen. To her pleasant surprise, the boys had used their pocket money to get her a birthday cake and had secretly organized a mini celebration for her. After the celebration, she texted Daniel to ask if he wanted to go on Skype with her that night. Daniel claimed he was working on his 3D design and would meet her on Skype within the next hour.

6:00pm PST

They connect via Skype. Daniel was sitting in his room cleanly shaved and smiling. He wished her a happy birthday and promised to celebrate future birthdays with her and the kids.

Jamie mentioned that the only thing she was worried about was that her ma would be uncomfortable about her relationship with him because they had only met online.

Daniel convinced her that everything would be okay, and he was going to be there real soon. "It's okay, just let your ma know I care a lot about you. And I would never hurt you. Can I talk to her? I want to get to know her better and give her some confidence in me. Mothers will want to see us doing good together. Talking to her might not be good enough for her. What is your mother's name?"

Jamie passed Daniel her mother's contact and name. Daniel sent a text introducing himself to Jamie's mother.

"Deal! I like that. Hey, please try to make a trip here and we can possibly spend Easter together ok?"

Their Skype conversation was cut off abruptly before Daniel could reply.

Immediately after their conversation got disconnected, Jamie received a text from Daniel:
"*Sorry, my Pearl, I lost internet connection here. :(*"

Before Jamie was able to reply the text, he called her on her mobile.

Daniel continued his conversation from where they had stopped. "Answering your last question on Skype before I lost you... Yes, that's a deal. I promise. Life without you is not worth living."

Both hung up, and Jamie started thinking about the conversation they just had. She felt she was on cloud 9, but her intuition told her to start giving some thought to this relationship that seemed too good to be true.

SEVENTEEN
Nip in the Bud

March 12, 6:00am PST

Jamie tried to call Daniel on his phone but was sent to his voice mail. She requested for him to return her call and as usual, he did so almost immediately.

In a caring tone, Daniel asked what was wrong.

"Last night I added the time zone for Belgrade, Prague, and North America to my clock in my phone... Then I realized both Belgrade and Prague are 8 hours ahead of Vancouver. You always tell me you are talking to your ma or Dejan, and I realized the time you talk to them are always in the wee hours of the morning. That got me curious... Sometimes, I text you to ask if we could talk, but there is always a window period which you can't because you claim you are talking to either of them, but that timing is early hours in the morning where they come from. I am not suspicious or anything. Just asking myself are we for real? I just don't want anyone to hurt me anymore. I don't think you will, but I have some fears and don't want us to act on impulse. I don't want to be a bother to you too, and I really am busy with my life as it revolves around my kids. I have picked up the pieces on my own, and my kids told me after my divorce, they never want to see me hurt by anyone anymore... I am only asking for your honesty and sincerity. Now I am falling in love with you, and I set aside my time and love for you because I am happy too. I only want to be sure we are for real cos I am really struggling here, but I have never told anyone. My life has changed over the past week. I am actually getting fearful. What if this is not real? I know I am strong, but there is only so much strength that I have left."

Daniel replied patiently, "Oh my Pearl, really? I was thinking something different. Do you think I'm not what I say I am? Awww. Now you're scared? I am so sorry. I know it's not easy. You are not being fair to me. I struggle to keep in touch with everyone. I talk with Dejan twice a day and sometimes with my mom. Had to make them all adjust because I need time for you. They are 5 hours away from me. My mom calls when she knows I'll be in, and she doesn't mind the time difference. Why all of the sudden did you become so critical and overly suspicious? I am doing my best to give my time to everyone. We talk at late hours too.

"Know what? I think we should take a break. Cos I don't know where this is heading. I've had almost no sleep at night since we met and you take it absolutely for granted. I just don't know what to say. I'm responsible for my actions, not how you choose to interpret them. It makes no sense to me. We are in touch almost 24/7. Except for a few hours and you can't trust what I do within those few hours we are apart? You don't even trust my intentions towards you. I'm just as innocent as you are in this. All I did was fall deeply in love with you. It makes no sense to me. I have no experience in dating online, and you told me you did not except for a few dates. If I'm not going to be trusted now for no good reason, there is really no need to go another step further. If I were a scammer like anyone else might think I am, I would not do so with my real identity. You know both these facts, but you can think negatively about me. I'm too nice, it makes us two because you are too good as well. You tell me what I want to hear, and I live for everything I have with you now. But I never worry because nothing is too good for me. What do you want from your life? What else could you possibly want? At this moment I am feeling a little dismayed, and I need to rest." Daniel explained.

Jamie hung up the phone. Feeling suspicious of Daniel gave her a sense of regret. But she reminded herself that she had to trust her gut and be strong. If it's meant to be, it will. Otherwise, she was still happy living her life revolving around her boys.

8.30am PST
Jamie arrived work, and received a text image of the bid he had won with Baker & Hughes. The one contract he claimed he had been working on for a while and had been talking a lot about and had been hoping to win the contract for. Jamie didn't bother to reply. She just felt happy for him and went back to her work.

4.00pm PST
Jamie arrived home after work that day to be greeted with a bouquet of roses on her table. She asked her kids who the flowers were from, and her son told her it was from Daniel.

The card was written as follows:
"To my Pearl, you are the reason I smile and why our love thrives across the miles. Happy Birthday, Dearest.

Love you forever,
Your loyal man... Daniel Slovák"

Jamie sent Daniel a text to thank him for the flowers.

Daniel immediately called her.
"I'm furious with the florist because they delivered the flowers one day late. I ordered them a week ago and meant to give you a birthday surprise. But they are one day late."

"It's ok, better late than never. Rest assured I am ok with this. It's the thought that counts."

"Okay, you are right. I was so disappointed yesterday. It was your birthday, and it was only right I got you something. I felt so bad when you got gifts from people at work and none from me. It didn't feel right, but it's okay now. I love you."

"I am glad you are back to your cheerful self again. Have a good day. I am sure you are elated after winning your bid for the job."

"I will be having further talks with the company Monday and will leave for Texas tomorrow. Hey, my Pearl... please don't leave me. You have given me hope, love and care. I don't want to talk about the conversation we had this morning. I didn't mean it when I suggested we go on a break. When I won this contract, I was overjoyed because it is going to be the turning point of my career, but at the same time, I felt a sense of regret for having suggested the break. I love you, and I realized I can't live a day without you anymore. Please my Pearl, give me a chance to prove my love to you. Please don't deny me."

Jamie's heart melted, and she relented. She was happy for Daniel and gave him the encouragement and support he needed.

David visited Jamie to celebrate her belated birthday. For the past 3 years, he would celebrate her birthday either a day earlier or later because he always reminded Jamie to celebrate her birthday on the actual day with her kids. She shared every bit of her new found friend with David. As he listened, he had mixed feelings. On the one hand, he felt happy for her as he noticed for sure she looked bright, cheery and very much happier. But he started to choke on his words as he told her he would always be there if she ever needed a shoulder to lean on. Jamie sensed an obvious jealousy and resentment David had towards Daniel, thinking this damn guy was intruding on their friendship. Jamie assured him no one would ever come between their friendship, and she gave David a tight hug.

"Whatever it is, just remember, if you ever need a shoulder to lean on, I'll always be here for you," he whispered to her in an assuring manner as she nodded with agreement. Both found it difficult to let go of each other.

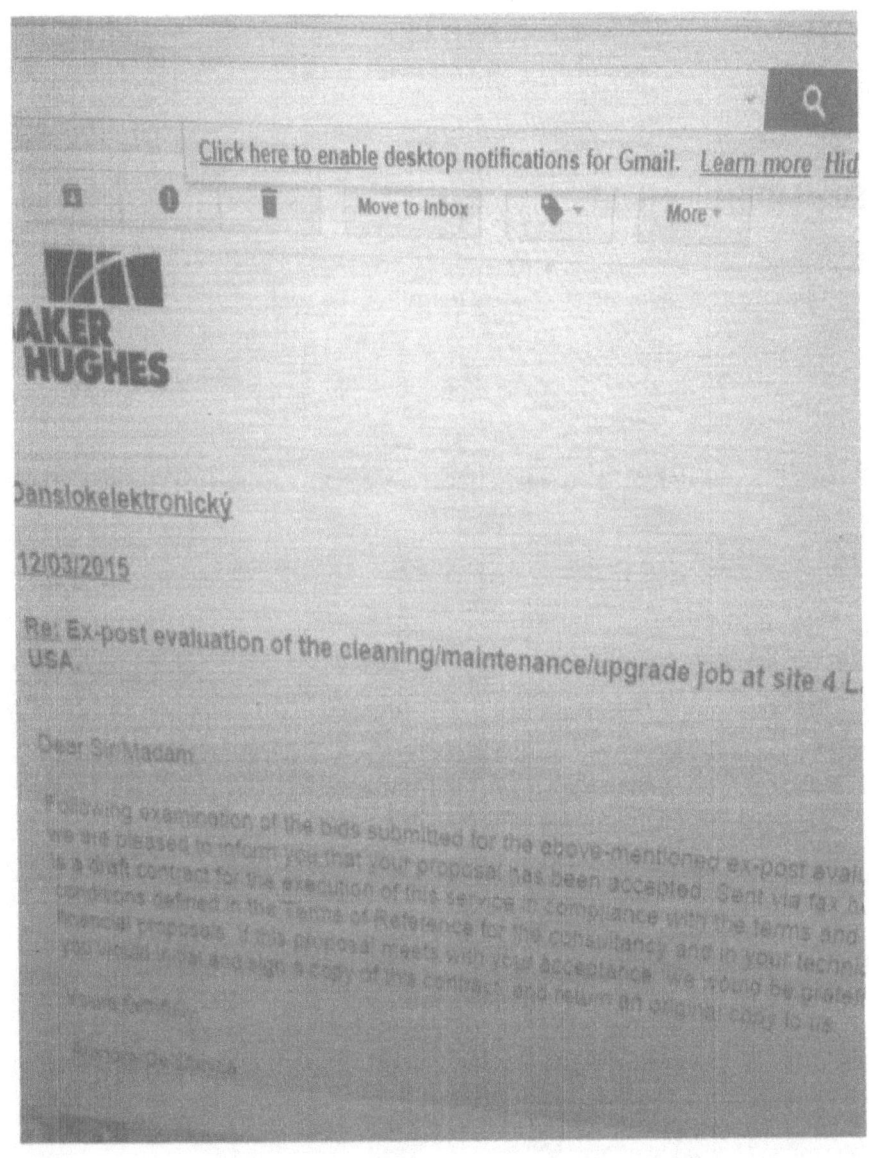

Screenshot of his email showing he had won a bid with a reputable company in Texas.

EIGHTEEN
Love in the Fast Lane

March 13th, 6:00am PST

Daniel informed her he was about to leave for Dallas, Texas soon.

"Safe journey. We'll talk later. Focus on the business first and get oriented with the place and company when you are there," Jamie replied.

"Yes, I will. Waiting to board the plane. Will call you for a few minutes. I'm gonna miss you so much..."

Two and a half hours later, Jamie received a text update from Daniel, *"Hey there, in Dallas now. How's your day so far?"*

"I'm doing well. Stay warm. I just checked the weather in Dallas, cloudy over there for the whole day. Take care and good luck with your meetings."

"Thanks, Pearl, I have found a hotel. Settled in, going to grab a bite. I'm starving. Pearl, this job is worth US$2. 9mil. With this, I want to give you and the kids a much better life. I'm a happy man now that I have you. All this while I have been thinking, Dejan doesn't need my money because his mother has a trust fund for him. I have worked so hard to win this contract because I want my work to be patented and do something good for myself. Now that I have you, at least making this money is worthwhile because I can share it with you and the family. This job is going to be quite demanding and will take a lot of my time for the next 10 days."

"It's ok, just focus on your work for the next whole week...we can talk briefly before we go to bed tonight. Please remember to have your meals. p.s. Aren't you afraid I might want to stick with you for the money now that you have disclosed the value of the job? Anyway, that's going to be your hard earned money so you do whatever you want with it. I don't really care about material wealth. Besides, you might need to reinvest in your business and to take care of your folks. Hey, no worries ok?"

"Alright, thanks. You are always so thoughtful. Another good piece of news I was planning to share with you. Dad came out from dementia today. Mom just got a hold of me to say the hospice is going to release him to go home for a week as he seems to be able to recall things. He suddenly asked about us. I think mom had been telling him about you every day. Pearl you must really be my lucky star. Why don't you talk to my dad and let him get to know you a bit? Will pass you his Skype and contact number later, okay? Meanwhile, I will work very hard to get this job fulfilled, and I want to meet you and the kids in Vancouver

once this is over."

Jamie welcomed the idea of getting to know Daniel's dad when he eventually got to go home. She assured Daniel to take everything one step at a time and to just focus on his job in Texas for now.

Daniel called Jamie to ask if she wanted to go on Skype. He said the internet reception in his hotel room was so poor, he was heading to the hotel lounge to Skype her. As he walked to the lounge, he described the setting of the hotel lounge to her. Saying that he felt as though he was in a tropical paradise. Then he set up his computer and hung up the phone after connecting with her via Skype. Jamie saw Daniel in a bright red T-shirt, clean and shaved. He looked so handsome and kept reminding her how much he loved her and was looking forward to giving her and the kids a better future.

"While I know you are planning to take good care of me and the boys, I know I will want to repay you in more ways... It's always better to give than to take. Always better to love than to be loved... Knowing you has made me feel overwhelmed with love, and I am afraid to become indebted to you."

"You have paid enough, and this is not about paying back, but about celebrating you as a person. You are a loving person, and you choose peace. Peace of mind is very expensive, but it can be cheaply acquired with a conscience powered by love."

"I am so afraid of you cos you are able to read me so well, and you seem to know my true self better than most people who have known me in my lifetime. Yes, I am peace loving, and I care a lot for others. That's how I am, and I don't feel stupid or anything negative. I just want to love and care for others. Life is not about materialism... It's about how we connect and do good. So our future generations will benefit from our good karma."

They continued their conversation for the next 5 to 10 minutes or so, and she suddenly lost him on Skype.

"My Pearl, sorry the PC went off. My battery died. Now it takes time to reboot it. I had better go to bed too since it's pretty late here. Is that ok?"

"Alright. Good night."

March 15th, 8:00am PST

Pearl, please add *dad's Skype username to yours. vy.slovák*
When you get to talk to him, please tell him he needs to rest ok? He has
been struggling with his health. I will need to use this whole weekend
to get ready for my meeting with the executives on Monday and start
making more contacts here.

11:00am PST
Jamie went online with Daniel's dad. She was only able to see him but couldn't
hear what he was trying to say. Vydra Slovák was an 80-year-old retired civil
servant who was originally from Prague. He had been battling respiratory health
issues, and Jamie could see the frail old man breathing through a tube sitting at
his desk with an oxygen tank next to him. Both Jamie and the Senior Slovák
tried to converse via Skype, but both attempts failed. Vydra texted Jamie on
Skype and turned off the video. He asked her about her life and said he wanted
to get to know her better. He claimed Daniel was his only child ever since he
lost his other child in a car accident. He described Daniel as a responsible,
loving and caring person and that he was happy that Daniel had found his future.
Vydra talked about regretting not having a big family and welcomed the idea
that Jamie had 3 kids. He was glad to know that his family was finally blessed
with more grandchildren and that his dream of having a bigger family was now
a reality. Vydra then went on to ask Jamie if she really loved and cared for his
son. He reiterated that Jamie will be the second woman Daniel had ever
introduced to his parents and hoped Jamie will not let his son down. Jamie
promised never to hurt Daniel and that she wanted to remain true to him. Jamie
had always been considerate and kind to others, and she knew Vydra just got his
memory back. She wanted to help Vydra keep his mind active, and so she asked
if he could teach her the Czech language. Vydra agreed and told her he would
teach her in a few days' time. After texting for almost an hour via Skype
messenger, Vydra told Jamie he was feeling tired and needed to go to bed. He
also told her he hoped to talk to her again soon.

TWENTY
Playing With Fire

March 16th 5:41am PST

"Good morning, my sweetest Pearl. How was your night? I am already at the venue. Your man is putting on a suit today... Next time I'll wear this on our wedding I think... I love you so much. Thanks for your wishes. Wish me luck at the meeting."

"I am sure you will do well. Didn't they say you have won the bid?"

"Yes, but still nothing concrete from them because there isn't any formal contract yet. We will finalize after meeting with the company's rep today. They are doing further due diligence and negotiations. Hopefully, we will get the deal completed today. Wish me luck."

8:00am PST

Daniel texted:
"Not looking good :("

"Have faith. Don't let anything drag your morale. Stay positive."

"I know, but I might lose this job. I'm unable to meet with lots of requirements so far."

"Just press on. It's your first time on a big project like this one. Have faith in yourself. Whether you win or lose this job, please don't despair. Use this experience to succeed the next time... Stay focused."

"It's basically about the completion guarantee and level of commitment once money is advanced to me. They need construction assurance that the job will be performed, and workers/material suppliers will be paid on time. They are working out an agreement with me, but on much stiffer terms because I am a one-man company. Anyway, I've got a way around it. We had two tricky scenarios which were for me to get a performance bond or an irrevocable bank letter of credit to cover whatever is advanced to me. The rest will be paid into an escrow account in my favor."

"No worries, as long as you managed to compromise with them on a solution, you are a step closer to getting this job done."

"I wasn't thinking too much about the payment. It was more about what if I needed more funds to finish this job. I have already invested all my savings in purchasing supplies and set aside some to pay my workers. I am hiring 8

contract staff to work on this project and will order my supplies from Germany."

"Just work around things. If you have set aside funds for whatever expenses you need to cover you should be safe, right?"

"Let's hope so, my Pearl. It's because I am putting in my entire savings and have taken a line of credit from my bank in Europe for this job. I just hope there will not be any surprises along the way."

"I trust you know what you are doing and would have gotten things planned and organized well. So just have more faith in yourself ok? I'll keep you in my prayers."

March 17th, 3:26pm PST

"Pearl, I received an advance by the company and managed to get the bank escrow opened with the balance. Trying to settle down at work. I will be at this site in Laredo for the next 10 days to work on this project. Once I am done, we will be whole. I love you.

I wish I could take photos of this place to send you, but I have signed a non-disclosure with the company, and photo taking is prohibited. I only managed to take a picture with my crew when we stood outside the site and had to rush to take a quick picture. :(

Please go check your email when you have time. I sent you something, and I look forward to sharing that with you."

Jamie received an email from Daniel. He had forwarded an email with an attachment containing an official Escrow statement from an ABN bank manager in charge of his Escrow account. The email read as follows:

> Hello Pearl,
>
> Here's our Alert ;)
>
> I love you. I'm at job site now.
>
> How's your day going?
>
> Your Loyal man
>
> Daniel.
>
> ****Forwarded Email below ****

Dear Daniel Slovák,

RE: Confirmation of Escrow Deposit.

This is to bring you up to speed with your escrow transfer. Attached herewith is the TT confirmation of deposit into your Escrow Manager Master Checking Account with Longrich UK.

Should you require any further clarifications, please do not hesitate to contact our customer service at Tel No 102-411-720.

Thank you for banking with us

Sincerely,

Lout Lapidaire.
Escrow & Settlement
Corporate & Institutional Banking
ABN Amro

Gustav Mahlerlaan 10 1082 PP Amsterdam The Netherlands
Tel: 102411720 Cable: ABN BANK Telex: 24455
SWIFT Dest: ABNCNL2AFRD

TRANSACTION ADVISE

Outward Telegraphic Transfer

```
                                   DATE: 17 MAR 2015
                                   OUR REF: 0016OT2370450
    001515                         YOUR REF: 14206070820
    BAKER HUGHES Co.               BENEFICIARY
                                   DANIEL SLOVÁK
──  #2929 ALLEN PARKWAY,
──  HOUSTON, TEXAS USA            A/C:4911340520
                                   BENEFICIARY BANK
                                   LONGRICH CITY BANK
──                                55 BRYANSTON ST MABLE ARCH TOWER
──                                LONDON, W1H 7AA
```

DETAILS OF PAYMENT

──

	AMOUNT		RATE	EQUIVALENT	
PRINCIPAL	USD	2,065,000.00	USD	2,065,000.00	
OT - Handling Comm			USD	N.A	
OT - Cable			USD	N.A	

SETTLEMENT MODE	A/C NO OR REF	TOTAL AMOUNT		
S1	129050608	USD	2,065,000.00	
S1	129050608	USD	N.A	

SETTLEMENT MODE	A/C NO OR REF	TOTAL AMOUNT		
S1	129050608	USD	2,065,000.00	
S1	129050608	USD	N.A	

PAYING BANK

CR

AS

Should you have any clarifications, please contact our customer service at Tel No
102-411-720 (for corporate customers).

THIS IS A COMPUTER ADVISE OUR SIGNATURE IS NOT REQUIRED

SETTLEMENT MODES
AA - SAVINGS A/C   AS - NAA   QW - QUICK
BI - CURRENT A/C   AC - ACV   CU - CASHIER 1 ORDER
VO - VOSTRO A/C   CS - CASH   CL - CLEARING RECIPT
CQ - CHEQUE

PADI ENTIRELY ABN-ABRO 15050 730OT230489 AKD/81015384/15101

ABN-AMRO

This was included as an attachment to the email he sent.

TWENTY-ONE
Friends With Benefits

March 18th, 7:00am PST

"I've put in an application to get my idea patented. Have a feeling this company will be interested in it. Lawyer told me not to commence work till I have submitted a patent application because the company might steal my idea and submit a patent before me. I need to work with an international law firm to get this arranged with my lawyer in Prague as well."*

"My cousin's a lawyer. I can ask him for you."

"If he deals with patents and trademarks, maybe you can ask him to recommend someone in the US. Otherwise, I will use the one which my lawyer in Prague has recommended."

8:30am PST

Another text came in from Daniel:
"Pearl I am finding it difficult to attach a document via email. I need to send my ID to the lawyer. He's got the application fee and all other documents. Can you try to attach with your device? Then send to my email address? Thanks"

Daniel took a snapshot of his passport and sent the image to Jamie's phone. Jamie helped attach and forward the image of his passport back to him via email.

"Done! Please check your email."

Daniel replied, *"Wow, how did you do that? Mine says incompatible attachment."*

"It's called a smart phone. LOL."

"A smart woman with a smart phone. I love that! LOL."

At break time, Jamie's gut feeling prompted her to check out the passport which Daniel had sent her that morning and attached a copy of the passport to the search bar in Google image. She conducted her investigations with her fingers crossed as if hoping his passport was not a fake because she still had reservations about this whole Daniel deal and thought things were just too good to be true. She even checked out samples of fake passports from Germany, Czechoslovakia, and other parts of Europe just to be extremely sure about this guy. Hope turned to joy when she didn't come across a single indication which might possibly suggest his passport was a fake. However, she did find it puzzling why he was holding a German passport rather than one from

Czechoslovakia, his country of origin.

Still unsatisfied with her findings, she decided to take her investigations another step further. This time, she ordered an identity search through Spokeo's people search engine to obtain a compilation of data from online and offline sources using Daniel's contact details. All Spokeo was able to discover was the phone number belonged to a company with not a single information which would lead to any connection to Daniel. She decided to save her questions to another occasion when she found an opportunity to probe further.

5:24pm PST

Jamie sent Daniel a text:

"Your dad's looking for you. He says it's urgent. He asked me to tell you they will be leaving for Belgrade to check what you asked for. I think you should give him a call once you are available. Your dad also says your mom told him she is not sure if they have enough $ so they will go to the bank to check first thing tomorrow morning. Hey, are you short of funds?"

"When did you talk? And how did he know about the funds? I discussed that with mom. That man is always eavesdropping."

"He Skyped me 15 minutes ago. He texted me on Skype to ask me to tell you they will head to the bank tomorrow to check."

"He is so nosey. He should be in bed by now too. Pearl, don't listen to him. It's ok, they will head to the bank to source for some funds for me. I need to pay for the patent rights application. I worked on a very tight budget. I have totally stretched every cent to make this job go smoothly. The patent demand came in unexpectedly and so I asked mom to look into her account. I have some funds in there as I had sent her a couple of months back. I could replace those funds once this job is over and the escrow is lifted."

Jamie's intuition warned her not to get involved with whatever financial issues he might face. After all, she had never met him in person. She quickly suggested that he should apply for a *line of credit*.

"I do have a line of credit, but I have maxed it out to make part of the payment for supplies. I do have things under control and will not need anyone else's help. So don't worry my Pearl. Everything will be ok."

Jamie felt relieved that he wasn't asking her for any financial assistance.

TWENTY-TWO
Action Plan

March 19th 9:00am PST

Jamie was greeted with the following text from Daniel

"Good morning my Pearl. How was your night?"

Jamie replied that she slept well and was happy to receive his text. Then asked if he had gotten his patent issue solved.

"Pearl it's not looking good. I won't start the job till I submit my patent application. The lawyer has requested I pay an advance of $23k as that's the cost of patenting my idea. He wants to at least obtain a patent pending number for me. My folks have managed to raise $9k for me, but I am short of $14k."

Jamie suggested Daniel should check with his bank or get another line of credit from them. Daniel said he already took the maximum from his line of credit in Europe for this job and had taken his entire savings to purchase the supplies. Whatever leftover he had now was enough to pay his staff at the end of the project. He had exhausted all sources of funds.

Jamie then recommended that he used his escrow account as collateral from the bank to get a new line of credit after all he didn't need that much. But Daniel told her he had tried that with his bank in Europe, yet they would not approve because he had already taken quite a huge loan from them. He asked her to think of a solution with him as he was getting stressed over this. He reiterated that his escrow containing the balance $2.1million would be released within 5 days of successful completion of the job, adding that he was looking forward to seeing her and the kids in BC immediately after the job was over. She decided to defy her intuition to do the right thing. She told Daniel she would loan him the US$14k he needed on condition that he returned it to her once the funds from his escrow were lifted.

Daniel kept asking the same question to confirm her decision, "Are you sure? I am not used to anybody helping me because I have been doing things myself all these years. I don't want to be indebted to anyone. And please allow me to sign an IOU because I want to honor returning you the loan once B&H releases the funds from the escrow account. In fact, I want you to manage the entire funds for me once it's been released. Save some for the kids' education and the rest for us. I really don't want to watch you suffer anymore and I only want you to let me take care of you for the rest of our lives together."

Jamie assured him she was positive about treating it as a business loan as long as he promised to return it to her. She told him she wanted him to finish his job so they could meet each other very soon.

He furnished her with a woman's bank account details in Massachusetts and Jamie changed her mind about transferring the funds. Jamie sent Daniel the following text:

"Sorry Daniel I am not comfortable wiring the funds to anyone else but you."

Daniel immediately called Jamie on her phone to clarify the matter with her. He explained to her that the lady she was sending to was an agent he had been using since he went to the U.S. to work. She helped with his taxes and remittances and now that he was stuck in Laredo, he couldn't possibly handle his bank transactions as well. He also claimed he had never opened a bank account in the U.S. and had been paying her a fee to do his accounts and transactions. He said she was trusted and even furnished Jamie with the lady's personal details. Jamie relented and wired the funds to him through the lady.

Daniel started working the next day claiming his lawyer was going through all the documents and would get the patenting done.

At the end of each day he would usually send Jamie a text to inform her of his job progress and remind her that his love for her was growing stronger by the day how much he missed her and that despite his hectic work schedule, he could never get her off his mind.

TWENTY-THREE
Self-Pity

March 25th

"Dad passed away *today. I am devastated."*

Jamie was shocked because it was only three days before that she last texted Daniel's dad via Skype messenger. And he did complain he was feeling tired and needed to rest more. She sent Daniel the following text,

"I am sorry to learn this. How is your mom taking it? Can I give her a call?"

"You may reach her at this number +420 228 882 446 but she doesn't speak a word of English and mom is a very timid woman."

"Do you plan on stopping what you are doing in Laredo and make a trip back to Belgrade for his funeral?"

"Pearl this is a big company, and I am committed to complete the job within the next 10 days, or else I need to pay a fine with each completion day delayed. I can't just leave the job for personal reasons. It will reflect badly on me and my company. They don't do things this way. Mom will be arranging to send my dad's body from Belgrade to Prague because it was dad's wish to be buried with the rest of our ancestors. Mom wants me to return for the funeral, and I promised her I will once this job is completed in a few days' time."

Jamie felt sorry for Daniel as she was sure he would be thinking about his late father and how his mom was coping alone in Belgrade.

She sent Daniel a text reminding him that she loved him and wanted to be there for him especially in such difficult times.

March 26th 5:00am PST

Jamie received a call from Daniel telling her he was going to be a little free today because his crew was doing the bulk of the job while he was waiting at the control room for his agent to provide him with updates on his supplies that had been scheduled to arrive from Germany. He told her everything should be at customs waiting for clearance, and his freight agent would be handling everything for him.

He asked Jamie if she was able to return to Prague with him to attend his dad's funeral and that his mom wanted to meet her as well. Jamie told him she would need to discuss that with her kids and would give him the answer thereafter.

That evening Jamie explained everything to her kids, and they agreed that she should go to Prague with Daniel. Jamie called her mom to ask if she was able to organize her annual trip to Vancouver 2 months earlier. Jamie's mom was retired and visited her and the kids each year. She usually spent 6 months with her grandkids and daughter in Vancouver and another 6 months with Jamie's brother's family in Hong Kong. Her mom agreed and was scheduled to arrive Vancouver by the end of the week.

TWENTY-FOUR
Cock & Bull

March 27th, 8:00am PST

Daniel called Jamie, sounding very upset. She assumed it was because of his dad's death that he was feeling so distraught. Daniel told Jamie he had a strong feeling his job was going to be delayed because the U.S. customs office had demanded additional duty to be paid for his supplies. Jamie asked to clarify, and he added, "Pearl my supplies from Germany are stuck at customs because some of the parts are not manufactured in Germany but in Taiwan. I have been ordered to pay an additional 10% in customs duty, and I am now stuck. It's a huge sum how am I going to get it?"

Once again Jamie started brainstorming for a possible solution with Daniel. Jamie asked him to contact the German distributor and demanded that they pay for it, but Daniel explained to her that he had already done that, and the distributor had told him to return them the goods if he didn't want them as they refused to bear the customs cost. Jamie kept suggesting other solutions, but every idea was shot down by Daniel. Finally, Daniel asked if Jamie was able to loan him another $48k to get this issue resolved. He promised her he would return the loan in full once he completed the job and got the escrow account lifted. He further explained to her that he just wished to complete this job and to go home to bury his dad. Jamie felt for him and decided to loan him the money. She told him this was all she would be able to do, and he had to honor returning her the money as soon as his escrow account was lifted. He kept thanking her for standing by him and promised to repay her with interest and take good care of her.

Just as she was about to ask him about his cell phone number, Jamie was interrupted by an alarm clock ringing over at Daniel's side. Instead, she asked why did he have an alarm set when it was night time over in Texas. Daniel explained that he lived his life organizing his day with an alarm clock. That alert from the alarm was to tell him he had to get out and check on his workers and had to hang up the phone then.

March 27th, 4:00pm PST

Jamie wired money to the same agent in the U.S. But this time to another bank account. Feeling a little curious, she asked Daniel why did she have to send funds to another bank account. Daniel explained that it was because the freight agent had an account with the same bank and didn't want any possible delays when it came to transferring funds to him. Daniel just wanted everything to be resolved and for his supplies to be released to him. Once customs cleared, it would take another two days to get them delivered to Laredo. Later that evening he sent Jamie a copy of the freight charges issued by the customs office.

March 28th, 7:00am PST

Daniel updated Jamie he had received the goods and was about to get busy with installations. Jamie went on with her usual routine.

As she was about to go to bed at night, she received a text from Daniel:

My Pearl, I am so exhausted right now, but I want you to know you are always on my mind. Thank you for helping me pull through this trying moment of my life. I thank God for giving me you. The job will be completed in 4 days' time, and once B&H lifts the escrow, I want to pass you most of the funds for safekeeping. I don't trust myself cos I love spending on luxury items. I need you to help control my funds, ok? I love you.

Daniel went on to text that he was looking forward to meeting her in about a week's time in BC, and they would finally get to leave for Prague together. He also told her that he had requested his lawyer to draft out a contract that promised Jamie she would own half of what he had in the escrow account once it'd been lifted upon completion of the job. He wanted to repay her for her help and to treat the deal as a business investment.

Jamie accepted the offer and turned in for the night.

March 31st 2:00pm PST

Daniel sent Jamie a text confirming that he and his crew had completed the job in Laredo and had run 3 tests to be sure the installations were flawless. He said he had finished packing his things and was scheduled to leave Laredo for Austin. He was feeling so excited to be with her the next day. He confirmed the following with her in a text message:

I should be meeting the executives in Baker & Hughes first thing tomorrow morning and hand over the report to them. Get them to sign off my job and fax the letter to release my escrow account. I will then confirm my flight ticket to Vancouver by tomorrow evening. I love you, my Pearl. Thank you for helping me make this project happen.

After reading that text, Jamie felt just as excited and started packing her luggage to get ready for her trip to Prague.

Apr 1st 9:00am PST

As usual, Jamie received a text from Daniel:

"Good morning my sweet Pearl. In less than an hour, we will become millionaires! Please send me a copy of your passport. I need to pass it to the travel agent to book our tickets to Prague. Love you."

64

That was the last message Jamie received from Daniel. She sent him a copy of her passport and never heard from him the whole day.

8:00pm PST

Jamie assumed Daniel must have been occupied with all the logistics and was busy getting ready to make his trip to Vancouver. She sent him a text asking how his day was. And received the following news:

"The company claimed they need to dispatch another quality control superintendent to the site with me before they can acknowledge successful completion of the work. I have to give them 3 days advance notice to book the superintendent. The earliest we can return to Laredo is next Tuesday because of the Easter weekend. Pearl, I am sorry for the delay. This is so frustrating. I have you waiting for me, a dad waiting to be buried, and a nagging mom who keeps reminding me about dad's funeral date."

TWENTY-FIVE
What A Load of Crap

Apr 2nd 10:00am PST

"Guess what? Dejan's mom sent me a text this morning wishing me success in our relationship. Of course, she meant it as sarcasm. She must have gone through Dejan's phone again," Daniel called Jamie to complain to her.

"Doesn't he lock his phone?"

"I should get him to do that. Anyway, we have nothing to hide from her. Just let her be. She is and will always be a spoilt daughter of a wealthy old man."

He then complained he was feeling so bored and lonely in Houston, how disappointed he was as he wasn't able to spend the Easter holidays with her and that he was feeling so worried not knowing how to deal with his mother who was expecting both of them back for the funeral by April 4th.

She tried comforting him and assured him that everything was going to be over in a few days' time. She tried to change the subject and asked him to look on the brighter side of life and to look forward to the days they were going to spend together. She used that opportunity to ask about his phone number. "Just out of curiosity, how much do you pay for your monthly cell phone bill?"

"The company in Maryland pays for it, so I don't have any idea about that. Why?"

"No, I just wanted to be sure you're not spending too much on the phone cause we can use Skype if need be."

"That's alright, my Pearl, the company has subscribed to an unlimited plan for us. You are always so considerate. I am grateful to have you in my life. Anyway, this apartment doesn't have WIFI connection so we can't use Skype and my stupid phone is so out of date I can't download apps like Skype. I think I should buy a new phone when I'm done with this job."

Daniel reminded Jamie how much he wanted to be with her there and then and that he was on the verge of giving up everything just so he could be with her and the kids. He further added, "If it weren't for the money, I would have just left this place, and we would have become whole by now."

For the next few days, Daniel sent Jamie text messages occasionally to remind her he was thinking of her and how much he missed her.

April 7th 7:00am PST

Daniel sent a text, *"Good morning, my Pearl. I can't wait to see you soon. Leaving for Laredo with the Superintendent soon. This final inspection shouldn't take too long. I am very confident about my work. I love you."*

Jamie smiled after reading that text message, sent him a reply wishing him good luck and was feeling so energized that morning. She left for work with high spirits. She couldn't wait to see Daniel, finally.

12:00pm PST

Jamie text Daniel at lunch time, *"Hey you... all set to get your ass over here? What time shall I pick you from YVR?"*

Daniel didn't respond to her text till 3:00pm PST

"They rejected the installations that were manufactured in Taiwan. They have demanded that I uninstalled those immediately and get them replaced only with German made ones. Pearl, I don't know what to do now. They wouldn't even release 10% of the funds from the escrow account to allow me to purchase the goods to replace. I am stuck. I have been spending the whole hour dismantling, and I feel so lost right now. I have sent an email to the dealership in Germany to have the goods replaced. I am waiting for them to respond. Pearl, please let me focus on the work first and let me handle this myself ok? I will text you later."

Jamie felt heartache for Daniel. All she was able to do now was to pray for him.

TWENTY-SIX
Bulls Never Run Out of Shit

April 8th 9:00am PST

Another fresh unpleasant update arrived and this time, the German distributor refused to exchange the products and replace them with German made parts. Instead, they had worked out a price difference, and he was required to pay the difference before they would warrant the exchange. He gave Jamie a quote of US$89K and told her how disappointed he was with the distributors for having sold him Taiwanese made parts and renege on sending him the German ones he had ordered from the start. He complained to her he had already run out of funds for this business and was not even able to complete his job as planned. He told her how worried he was now claiming that Baker & Hughes might not honor the full payment to him as he was now stuck with nothing. He kept reiterating how frustrated he was feeling and how he had disappointed her and his parents.

Jamie told him she would help him one last time, but he really had to return her everything once he completed the job successfully and got the escrow lifted.

"Daniel, I really have nothing else left once I send you this last one. I really need your assurance that this is the final one because there is no way I can help anymore. Besides, you will need to return me the full loan once you get the funds from escrow lifted. That's all I have left for my kids."

April 9th 4:00pm PST

Something in her kept telling her to stop helping him financially. She defied her inner soul as she kept thinking about his dead father waiting to be laid to rest. She thought of how both their futures depended on him completing that job so he would be able to get his escrow account lifted and repay her the loan she had helped him with. Jamie transmitted the final sum to cover the installations hoping in her heart that this Baker & Hughes job would be completed quickly, and they would soon become whole.

April 11th 2:00pm PST

He forwarded her pictures of about 8 boxes containing installation parts that had just arrived from the first shipment that the German distributor's agent in the US had dispatched from a company in Texas. He let her know that he would be very busy installing the parts one by one on his own for the next few days. He commenced his task and for the next 8 days, he would text Jamie to send his love to her every 8 hours between breaks and to update her with his job progress. Sometimes he would complain to her how exhausted, he was from lifting the German parts and explained to her how much heavier and solid the equipment was compared to the ones from Taiwan.

April 19th 6:00am PST

Daniel called to notify Jamie that there had been a breakdown between the German receiver's relationship with the Main distributor. The receiving customer wanted to re-wire the funds back to Jamie's account, and Jamie was to re-transmit the funds directly to the American dealership. Jamie called the German bank manager to send them instructions to have her funds returned to her account in Vancouver, but the manager refused to entertain her. Nothing was being done in Germany.

She felt so helpless, and she really wished she could fly to Texas to lighten his workload at his job site.

Just then David called to meet for dinner, and Jamie shared the whole story with her friend.

"Wow, he seems to have one problem after another coming from this job. The big guys never make it easy when they award a large job to a proprietor. Something he should have been prepared for. It seems he is quite an amateur, eh?"

"I feel bad for him, though. And now with his late father waiting for him to be back in Prague to bury him...." All Jamie was able to think about was the tough life Daniel was going through at that point.

"Well, whatever it is my dear, just don't invest in his business," he cautioned at Jamie sheepishly, then realized his warning might have been too late, as she ignored his last sentence. "Did you?"

"Did I? Hell no..." Jamie lied defensively and looked away.

April 25th 8:00am PST

Daniel called her about the bank issue with Commerzbank, Germany. And that he was desperate because he had just received an email from the American dealership that they demanded their goods be uninstalled and returned to them as they still had not received their funds from the German agent. He forwarded the email to Jamie.

On Sat, Apr 25, 2015, at 6:54 AM, Floyd Watson

25-4-2015

Mr Slovak

OBJECT: RETURN OF SUPPLIED INSTALLATIONS.

Dear Sir,

We sourced for your contact information from Mr. Bertrand K. (7405132530) who we are instructed is your Agent in Germany. An attempt to reach you on phone proved abortive. On April 18th 2015 acting on directives from your contact in Germany we made a supply of certain electrical installations to you in Laredo TX.

At the time of the order, your agent held an on-sale contract for the goods which required delivery interstate within five (5) days and so far we have fulfilled our end of this agreement to the extent of the delivery to you.

In a conversation with your agent early this week we were instructed that there is a course of conduct between your agent and the party in Germany and that there has been a collapse in the relationship structure causing a delay in funds getting to us. Our initial request for the immediate return of the installations was met with a promise to be paid in full on or before Friday this week citing that they were already installed by you.

We'd like to express our utmost disappointment as we had explained earlier to your agent that we will not entertain any failure on his part to make remittance for the installations supplied at the stipulated time. My wife and I injected our entire savings to start this business, we cannot survive with such a huge deficit sitting on our balance sheet.

My wife and I have come to a conclusion to retrieve the supplied installations (freight at our cost) if payment totaling $33,115.00 is not made available to us on Monday 27 April 2015.

Please advise,

Best Regards,

Floyd Watson

630-473-3495

Sent: Saturday, April 25, 2015 at 1:53 PM

70

From: "Daniel Slovák"

To: "Floyd Watson" <floyd.watson@fastservice.com>

Cc: "Jamie"

Subject: Re: Installations.

Hello Floyd,

This is to confirm receipt of your email and so sorry for your inability to reach me on the phone. I tried countless times to contact you on the telephone as well. I'd like to start off by tendering my sincere apologies for the delayed payment which is by no means intentional on our part. Find attached a copy of the bank slip evidencing full payments made by my wife in Canada to Mr. Bertrand in Germany. I reiterate that the delay was not intentional, and we are very straight forward business people. This most unfortunate delay as you know is as a result of a breakdown in dealings with ACS control systems. The German dealership as they have been most unreasonable and unreliable from the start. My wife and I are the process of retrieving the funds paid and we have been guaranteed by Mr. Bertrand and the bank to get this next week. My wife and I have decided to deal with just one dealership, and we are very ready to do this with you if given the chance, which is just a few more working days to make not just this payment but to do further business with you in time to come.

I hope my request meets with your high consideration.

Best Regards,

Daniel Slovák.

Date: Saturday, April 25, 2015

Hello Daniel,
I appreciate your response to our concerns but an appeal alone is insufficient at this point. We don't have an existing relationship with you, and the contract we had with Mr. Bertrand is now invalid.
The decision to contact you resulted from heated deliberations between my wife and I aimed at saving our business, we'll be more comfortable doing business with you when the cost of the installations supplied is remitted.
As for now our decision to retrieve the installations on Monday stands.
Best Regards,
Floyd Watson
XXX-XXX-XXXX

These string of emails were the ones that started to trigger Jamie's suspicions because she simply couldn't believe that any legitimate business would want to cancel a business relationship just because of a US$33K deal. This prompted her to conduct more investigations on the email extension fastservice.com. To her horror, she was brought to a webpage confirming that fastservice.com had been used by scammers. It was at this moment, she realized she hadn't checked the Tineye website using all the photos she received of Daniel. She started uploading pictures of him she had in her possession, and she almost had a heart attack when the site confirmed all the photos had been stolen from the website and Facebook page of a prominent spiritual marketer who was based in California. Completely devastated and frantic, heart pounding fast and legs shivering as she broke down in tears and sank into her chair, her mind went blank. She was so certain that she had been a victim of a romance scam. Her mind started to only think about how she had let her kids down and that they were going to be left with nothing.... Penniless and homeless.

At that point, all she could hear was Tammy's voice, warning her over and over again about all the pointers she had shared while dining together at the restaurant. Jamie covered her ears and bowed low in shame, crying uncontrollably. "Why didn't I see all these coming?"

TWENTY-SEVEN

What's Up Next?

April 25th 1:00pm PST

Her mind kept rewinding as she recollected how convincing Daniel had been. She started playing back every single event that had occurred and went through all his text messages, emails and pictures sent out. Crying hysterically, her hands shivering as she unfolded more and more truth from the pieces she put together. Confusion turned to desperation as she asked herself a string of questions. "Should I lodge a police report? Should I talk to the bank? Oh God, please tell me what should I do!" She felt her world had collapsed, she looked back at her happy life as she ushered in the new year, moved out of her old home, got her new address and phone number yet her life was still cursed, ending up with yet another perpetrator. Worst still, this time, she lost everything she had.

If for any reason, you ever need a shoulder to cry on, just give me a shout, and I will let you lean against mine. The voice of David was what she could hear whispering in her ears over and over again. She decided to send David a text.

"Hey, Dave, are you available to meet me?"

It didn't take long for David to reply, "Sure. I'm at the gym right now and should make it to your place in about an hour. You want me to stop by and get you?"

"Yes, please! Thanks."

The minute she saw David approaching her complex on his motorbike, she rushed up to him, gave him a tight hug, and tears flooded down her face followed by her uncontrollable cries. For a moment David just wrapped his arms around her, not uttering a single word, puzzled at whatever was going on.

David took Jamie to Horseshoe Bay where they found a nice refreshing spot by the water. Still oblivious to what had transpired, he just sat on the bench as he waited patiently for Jamie to reveal what was actually going on. He started making guesses to himself in the dead silence between the both of them which was occasionally interrupted with children laughing by the playground nearby or seagulls flying above them, but it was all white noise. "Could it be, perhaps, that his best friend may have just broken up with her boyfriend? Or the worst case scenario... did she gets cheated by the guy?" His mind kept wandering.

"I've been scammed very badly," Jamie said breaking the awkward silence between them as she poured out her sorrows, "I've been catfished. Daniel Slovák is just a fictitious character."

David got so confused his thoughts flying out of his mouth unfiltered, "Scammed? Catfished? What the hell's going on? What are you talking about? What's catfished?"

"Daniel is not Daniel after all. A bunch of perpetrators are behind the scam."

Jamie started explaining the true meaning of being a victim of a catfish. That the perpetrators had used someone else's profile as bait to hook on to its victims.

David calmed Jamie and decided to inspire her with a story which happened to one of the most important women in his life some 30 years ago. He never expected he would ever see history repeat on another woman he loved. His mother was also a single parent then, in her early 40s bringing up 3 kids, and was scammed horribly by a man who claimed to be her financial advisor. She had been swindled of about $350k and had to put a smile on her face to hide her troubles from her kids while she picked up the pieces by herself and started their lives all over again.

He hoped to inspire her with a true story and to remind her to protect the kids by not letting them know anything about the whole episode. Besides, he wanted to sprinkle her with a ray of hope, like his mom, she would eventually come out from this nightmare a tougher woman and would do well.

"What's crucial is you start recollecting the entire encounter you had with those pieces of shit. Record everything down and compile whatever evidence you might have. Then make a trip to the RCMP and file a report. You told me he had this job going on in Laredo. Why don't we contact the company to confirm your suspicions?"

"No, Dave. I am positive. Laredo is just part of the story they have fabricated."

"They? Who're they?"

"The group of scammers! They work as syndicates and operate from different parts of the world. Some are in the U.S., some of their accomplices are in parts of Asia, Nigeria, everywhere! Which reminds me they are in the U.S. because I received a copy of Powerball tickets."

"Ok, let's not alert him you have discovered you've been duped. Keep playing the same tune and behave normal till we can get more clues from them. Meanwhile, I'm going to speak to my contacts on searching for IP addresses, exedra. Have you lodged a report with the authorities?"

Jamie shook her head and added, "I've no clue what to do at this stage. You're the only one I've spoken to about this."

"Well, document the whole plot and string of events that have taken place with this Daniel fellow. Then immediately go to the RCMP to lodge a report. Please, let's not delay this whole issue."

4:00pm PST

She started recording the chain of events that had happened. Halfway through writing, her twins entered the room and interrupted her, "Mom, did you forget it's our birthday today, and we're supposed to head somewhere to celebrate?" Jamie paused her work and embraced her twins so tightly, wished them a happy birthday, and cried, "I love you. I'm sorry."

After taking her kids out for an early dinner, Jamie dropped them off at a bowling alley and headed to the RCMP to lodge a police report. She sought their help to contact the German bank to inform them of the scam and also to instruct the latter not to release the funds to the receiving party in Germany.

The RCMP constable in charge of her case was away on training for the whole week. Jamie became desperate looking for relevant authorities to assist. The RCMP front desk personnel claimed that hers wasn't classified as an emergency case, instructed her to speak to her constable in charge and to wait for his return.

While all these were taking place, Daniel sensed Jamie had been reacting differently as she delayed replying his texts and didn't answer his calls. He resorted to calling her mom instead to get a hold of Jamie. Still trying to maintain her composure, she played along with him.

April 26th
11:00pm PST

Jamie called the bank in Germany herself, discovered her money was locked in a bank account and with a little good fortune; a suspicious bank manager had put a hold on the receiver's account. That infuriated the accomplice trying to withdraw or transfer the funds to where he got arrested. The bank claimed they had handed the case over to the German police. She asked if the receiving customer was really being held in police custody but the bank refused to comment on that.

April 27th
8:00am PST

Jamie rushed to her bank and instructed the manager to close her account and establish a new one because the perpetrators had her bank details and identity. The bank put her account on high alert citing a possible case of identity theft. She then got her bank manager to write to the German bank to notify them of her new bank details and requested that her funds were legitimate as they appealed to them to seek their assistance to have her funds rewired back as soon as possible. As she connected the chain of events together, she realized why he was interested to know her mother's maiden name. That was a crucial piece of data banks kept on record and was a question they'd ask bank customers whenever they needed the account holder to verify ownership of the account.

With no updates received from any authorities, anxiety turned into desperation. She started contacting the FBI, the Singapore police force, and Interpol. The FBI took 3 days to revert back to her, and all they could tell her was to submit her report to another agency called IC3. The Singapore police force was prompt with their reply. Within half an hour, Jamie was connected with the Commercial Crime Department and assigned an officer in charge of her case. He contacted her immediately and asked for full details from her. He made it clear that because the scam happened while in Canada, it was not within the jurisdiction of the Singapore law enforcement officers to be involved, and he would have to close the case. However, because such romance scam cases had become so rampant over the past 2 years, he wanted to file the whole report, document it and submit it on her behalf to Interpol first thing the next morning. This was worse than a nightmare.

Jamie disguised herself as Carol and created a new profile on the various dating portals. Within minutes on Tinder, she saw the perpetrator online once again and alerted the authorities as well as the dating site. She told them they were now a step closer to getting the culprits since they could trace their exact location, tip Interpol and get them busted. The only reply she got from Tinder was that they claimed they would cooperate only if the relevant authorities were to contact them. Once again it seemed that her pleas had been ignored and over ruled with bureaucracies.

Over the next few days, Jamie spent her time researching and writing to all relevant authorities. She made sure the RCMP officer was kept in the loop in all her correspondences. She received an email from the scammer whom she encountered the first time in August 2014 with just two words– Good Job – which sent shivers of fear down her spine. It finally hit her that the scammers were from the same group all along. They didn't get her the first time when they met through Ashley Madison, but they managed to do so through Tinder. She felt her world shattering, and she felt so dumb to have fallen for their ploy. As she recollected her encounter with Daniel, she realized why Daniel knew her ethnic roots when he first went online with her. She knew that the scammers were aware she was careful with facts and they actually sent her all the documents to satisfy her curiosity. Daniel's passport, the letter from ABN AMRO with the escrow account details, details from the organization which he had won the bid. She was now certain she had been their target all along and had the whole event well-orchestrated.

She was certain she had been under the radar of the same group of perpetrators since last August. They had been watching and profiling her because they had their story fabricated so well and the whole plot had been carefully planned.

Tired of waiting for any further action by the authorities and desperate to recover her life savings, she left her twins in her mother's care and set off to Maryland in search of the store in which Daniel had purchased a lotto ticket which he had attached as a document to her via Skype. She took a closer look at the lottery ticket and burst into tears after scrutinizing the ticket in detail, discovering that the ticket was in fact purchased in North Carolina and not from Maryland where Daniel claimed he was initially. "Why didn't I notice that when I was trying to confirm these things about him right from the start?" She chided herself for having been so negligent.

Over the next few days, as she frantically got in touch with all the relevant authorities, she knew her chances of getting her money back or even getting the perpetrators caught were drawing closer to zero. She decided to fight back on her own.

By now, she had lost all hope of getting any results from the bureaucracies imposed by both the Canadian and American authorities and decided to take the matter into her own hands.

The lottery tickets which Daniel claimed he had bought for her on Mar 11th

TWENTY-EIGHT
An Eye for an Eye, Tooth for a Tooth

May 1st

She arrived after three long days of driving and having slept in her Odyssey disheveled and sore from two nights sleep inside the van. She arrived to find the town looking much like any other she had driven through to date and was a bit disappointed that it looked so average, hardly the place to find these guys she thought to herself as doubt sank into the pit of her stomach that this whole desperate excursion was simply a further waste of time and money. The day was early and to shake off her doubt and despair she decided a breakfast and a strong coffee were in order. She decided on a small café just across the street from the store where the lottery ticket was purchased. She sat down to order checking through her emails and to her surprise she discovered that she had finally received an update from the German authorities. She now learned from the German prosecutors that they were investigating the case as there was strong possibility that there were more than one victim involved in the case. They also claimed to have salvaged some of the funds she had sent and informed her that they would not be able to release the money back to her till they had completed the case in which they had been cooperating with Interpol as well. She now had mixed feelings. She felt relieved that they had managed to salvage more than half of the funds but at the same time frustrated they couldn't divulge much to update her on the case. She found the local paper on the counter and read the front page, thumbing through it to see what, if any news there was about fraud crimes in the area. But there was nothing, just stories about angry dog owners not being able to walk off leash in the park nearby, nothing that would hint of a fraud gang, *Hopeless, damn fuss this was,* she thought as her coffee arrived and she gently took a sip. She put down her cup to let it cool and a customer at the door caught her gaze, an older man bending down to talk to a young boy asking some questions but something odd grabbed her attention, the second boy out of view of the old man coming from behind him and stealing his wallet, *Oh crap,* she thought and almost charged out to stop them then thought, *damn my purse, my breakfast!* She turned to grab her purse and then back at the boys who were already heading down the street, she promptly pulled out some cash and handed it to the hosts and said, "I have to run!" then bolted for the door. Upon reaching the old man, she thought *I have to follow these boys*! And rather than get waylaid with discussion, smiled politely at the man as she passed him on her way out the cafe.

She soon caught up with the two boys who were unaware of her following them. She was relieved they had not noticed her. They headed to a lane, and she stopped for a second and thought, *What now...should I?* knowing full well the chances that something bad might follow she pondered but quickly her gut filled with desperation and she thought, "What if these two can lead me to the gang, if such a gang exists?" She stepped forward in earnest pursuit. As lanes went she thought this one wasn't a bad one, not too dirty or scary looking just a few garbage cans and loading docks all things you would expect to see in a lane, even the graffiti seemed to conform to some modesty she thought as she shadowed the two boys down the lane, still trying to convince herself this was not a bad idea.

For a second, she thought she lost the boys. They seemed to have vanished when all she did was look in another direction for a moment, then she heard the familiar click of a door latch locking to her right just about where she had last seen the two. She ran for the door hoping it had not locked behind them and was refreshed when she put her thumb on the latch and the bolt retracted.

"Got it!" she mumbled.

The door half opened, and she peered inside fearing the boys might be too close, but she saw an empty tiled floor corridor with doors on each side and no sign of the boys, She didn't hear another door and reminded herself that she needed to pick up the pace, she was losing them. She hastened down the hall looking for an open door or room. The hallway turned to the left, and she thought she could hear the click of the boys shoe heels on the floor as she rounded the next corner. Down the hall appeared to be an open office area with some desks, but the lights were off, and the area was dimly lit with a bit of daylight from an apparent window nearby. She was less sure of what to do next since there were so many places now to go. She knew there were more people about by the random sounds coming from around the office, but could not make out how many or where they might be. She became concerned she would run into someone, but thought to herself that all she had to do was be polite and explain that she had simply followed the boys after what she had observed. The office looked entirely professional and clean, and she was beginning to think this was less likely a gang and more likely a couple of boys off to see an older brother when she felt a sharp crack on the back of her head and brief flash of white light before falling forward toward a wall. She reached out to break her fall, but everything was going dark so fast she could only make out a pair of Nike sneakers as darkness and unconsciousness finally consumed her.

TWENTY-NINE
Rock Bottom

"You stupid bloody ass, what the hell were you thinking bringing her here?"

"You're always telling me not to think cos it's dangerous when I think, so I bring her here, then you can tell me, that's all. You want me kill her? Fine, I do that, fuck. She was a fucking pain in the ass to bring to," Jas replied frustratedly.

"You call that skinny bitch heavy? Wow, you're getting fucking lazy! You shit, maybe I should pop your sorry ass, Fuck! Can you do anything right?" Rachel asked Jas impatiently, Jas had faithfully worked for the company since he was a kid.

Rachel was a 6-foot-tall, slender Caucasian lady, in her late 20s, who had inherited the multimillion dollar organization from her father after he died of a heart attack a few years back. Affiliate Syndicate leaders from the underworld were pretty apprehensive about her taking over the empire due to her lack of experience and exposure to the world of money laundering, indirectly funding acts of terrorisms, and a whole list of criminal misconducts. However, nobody was aware that as she had grown up fast, she had learned a lot about the business from her father whenever she spent time with him.

"Boss you know I hate it when you say dis' shit?"

"Well don't be such a fuck ass, holy fuck! My whole afternoon is gone for this shit; I don't have time for this right now…"

"Fuck! Ok, I'll kill her and take and dump the bitch."

"No. We need to know who she is first and what she was doing in the office following the boys."

Jas led Rachel down the hall to the freezer room where Jamie had been bound and chained to the wall with a black sack placed over her head. Jas opened the freezer compartment door, and Rachel looked to the end to see Jamie chained to the wall and unconscious on the floor. She walked up and lifted the dark hood on her head enough to grab Jamie's ear and gave it a sharp, hard twist, nothing, not even a twitch, Jamie remained motionless and unconscious.

"Well you certainly gave her a whack on the back of the head, Jas, that should have woken her up."

Rachel heard Jamie breathing and by the cool-warmth of her skin, was certain she was still alive.

"You must have given her a hell of a smack Jas because she is totally out."

Rachel checked the back of Jamie's neck and head and found a bruising and swelling at the base of the skull.

"Well, that's not looking too good," Rachel said as she lifted the hood to get a look at Jamie's face, she lifted the eyelids to check for signs of burst blood vessels and noticed her right eye was blood red.

"Jas it looks like you gave her one hell of a blow, her right eye looks worse than her left one so there is going to be trouble with this one when she wakes up. You might have hit her a bit too hard."

"Let's kill her then!" muttered Jas.

"No!" replied Rachel, "Not till we know what's going on. Keep her locked up and I will see what I can find out about this woman, did you bring her purse?"

"Yep, I'll get it."

Rachel rummaged through her purse and found Jamie's passport, "Canada? What the hell is a tourist doing following the runts? Hmmm, I bet she saw the kids stealing and followed them like some do-gooder. Fuckin stupid Canadians, they've got to be the dumbest bunch of clowns on the planet. Well, I'll look this bitch up and see what's up. In the meantime, you keep her out till then. Just don't whack her on the head anymore, I've got a hunch this one's going to be a bit messed up when she comes around."

"What do I do when she wakes up?" asked Jas.

"Put a bucket in the freezer I don't want her peeing on the floor, it's a bitch to get the smell out later, call me when she wakes up."

***

Carol was awoken by the sound of her alarm clock ringing, she looked up at the ceiling trying to connect the entire ordeal from her nightmare. She was now certain of her true identity, confirmed that Rob was actually David, and was finally aware how she had ended up with the Syndicate.

THIRTY
BACK TO REALITY

As David made his way on his motorcycle, he started developing several possible hypotheses on how his beloved Jamie could have possibly ended up as Carol. What could she be doing in North Carolina, communicating with people on Tinder although she had sworn to him she would never ever go near online dating portals ever since she was stripped of her own identity and livelihood.

Knowing how resourceful Jamie was, the first thought that came to his mind was *She could have possibly found some clues which had led her to the perpetrators,* he thought to himself. *Or perhaps she had been kidnapped by those scumbags*!

"Fuck! I wish I had a crystal ball that would give me all the answers. I have a strong feeling this is going to be hell'a perplex because it was puzzling to know that she seemed to be suffering from memory relapse or something."

He approached a gas station, filled up the gas tank, and checked his Tinder account hoping to receive more updates from Jamie. This time, there was no message from her, and he decided to send her one instead.

"Hey, Sweet! It's me again. Which part of North Carolina are you at? I hope to meet you soon."

He paused for a while, hoping to receive a reply from Carol, but there was nothing coming from the other end.

"Sweet, I'm going to find you and rescue you. Meanwhile, just try finding out more about stuff like where your actual location is, but go along with your daily chores. Be on your guard throughout ok?"

He was beginning to feel worried for her safety and before he got on his motorcycle, he sent her one last message, sounding a little desperate, *"Please reply as soon as you get this. I will find a way to save you."*
With that, he logged off to continue his journey to his final destination.

Over the next few days, Jamie started plotting her escape as she secretly kept in contact with David. She tried finding her location on Google maps, but the Syndicate had all access to Google blocked, making it impossible to locate their whereabouts. Her plot to escape took a toll on her job performance, and both Jas and Rachel began noticing that something was clearly distracting her.

"You managed to find out your actual location?" David text Jamie.

"No."

"I don't understand how your distance away from me on Tinder hasn't changed one bit although I've been travelling nearer and nearer to North Carolina. When I was in Vancouver, you were apparently 29km away from me, and now you are still 29km away. This is absurd," came David's text.

"They hacked the distance tracker, Dave. They have software that allows them to manipulate the distance from their match on Tinder and various dating portals so the victim always thinks the one they have been matched with is somewhere nearby. Because of this tracking software, sometimes I am matched with someone from the U.K., And he'd think I'm also from the U.K."

"It's best you'd delete all our messages cos we never know if they are reading anything here," suggested David.

As Carol did her routine, deleting all communication with David frantically, Jas appeared out of nowhere, snatched the phone from her and started reading what was left of the message between David and Carol.

"What the Fuck? Who the fuck is Rob?" Jas asked Carol. "Why did you delete the messages with him when you know you had to keep all messages for us to check on a random basis? What's going on here, Carol?" Jas grabbed on to Carol's hair and pulled her head back forcing her to look him in his eyes, "Huh?"

"Rob is a new flame. He wants to meet me before he sends me anything," Carol explained. "And..."
Before Carol was able to defend her stand, Jas received another message from Rob.

"Carol, you there?"

"Yes, darling. I'm here. What's up sugar pie?" Jas replied on behalf of Carol.

Rob left the conversation as he was immediately aware that wasn't Jamie's writing style. For one, he was certain, Jamie would never use the words 'darling' or 'sugar pie' and now that he was sure Jamie had finally regained her memory, he was certain it was impossible that she would write that way. "Fuck. I hope she's fine," he exclaimed, he had to find her, it was all he was concerned about at that moment.

Jas sent Carol to Rachel and handed her phone over to the woman. "Carol, Syndicate, is very tech savvy, we have been monitoring your phone line all these while. Please enlighten us about this Rob guy."

"He's just another guy who is interested in a relationship. The usual stuff, Rachel," Carol replied confidently. Carol was sure despite how tech savvy they were, that Rachel would have addressed her as Jamie or Rob as David from the beginning. However, as she was still trying to fish out information from her, she was sure they had no clue about David or that she was gradually regaining her memory.

"Jas, from now on you will take over Carol's task. I'd like her to work on other smaller projects as I need her to assist with Bertrand's case soon," Rachel instructed Jas while looking at Carol.

"Why don't you let me finish off what I have started with him?" Carol interrupted, hoping to get a chance to alert David about the current situation they were in.

"Nope, you don't need to worry about this Rob guy anymore. Leave it to Jas after all Rob won't know the difference anyway."

Rachel made it clear she didn't want Carol to have anything to do with Rob. Carol, who was now aware of her true identity, tried hard to hide her disappointment as she was certain she was going to lose David once again.

She knew she had to continue to play the same tune with members of Syndicate. She was now entrusted to perform mediocre tasks such as putting up fake property listings on Craigslist, Kijiji, and other online classified ads platforms to scam people of their money. Once again, Jas had to show her the initial ropes on how they used a robotic software to place classified ads all over the internet to scam new victims. Though her work seemed menial, she had much more following up to do with potential tenants who fell for her property listings. Though she was forced to cease contact with David, she was pleased that given her new role, she discovered a way to gain access to Google maps and so she managed to progress with her investigations as she was desperately trying to find her exact location and to plan her escape.

Meanwhile, Jas tried getting to know Rob better, but Rob was cautious with who might be chatting with him at the other end and decided to play along with Jas.

"*Carol, shall we meet?*" Rob asked.

"*When, darling?*" Jas replied as he started to check out what Carol had written under her profile. He suddenly flew into a rage when he noticed that Carol had used her own picture to lure new victims. *What the fuck are you thinking?* He thought to himself as if questioning Carol. *I'm gonna fuck this bitch for using her real image. Dumb fucker!*

"*Tell me where and when I'll be there for you my love,*" Rob played along, hoping to get a hint of where the other party was.

Jas obviously had no intention of telling Rob where they were and was only interested in scamming the guy of his savings. He kept sharing his pathetic life as Carol, explaining that she hoped Rob would bail her out of her credit card debts.

Rob, on the other hand, was certain he wasn't communicating with Jamie but didn't want to lose communication with the perpetrators as that seemed like the only clue he had that could bring him closer to Jamie. That night Rob tossed and turned on his hotel bed, unsure how he would be able to save Jamie from the perpetrators. He thought to himself that the only way he could probably save Jamie was to seek the assistance of the FBI in North Carolina. He checked the internet to find the nearest FBI agency in the area and decided to check out from his hotel immediately to start his journey to the FBI agency in Charlotte, North Carolina.

THIRTY-ONE
The Next Attempt

David arrived at the FBI building in Charlotte, North Carolina, and was filled with hopes that he was getting closer to saving Jamie. At the agency, he showed his phone to an officer in charge of his case and asked if they had a department that would be able to crack the location for Carol's whereabouts. He was given one piece of bad news after another. First, they told him he had no case as they did not have any jurisdiction to deal with cross border scamming cases. Then they instructed him to file such cases with the Internet Crime Complaint Center or the IC3.

"My friend's life is in danger. What the hell?" Dave reacted angrily. "Inspector, can we contact the online dating site to get their cooperation then? I've written to Tinder's feedback unit the day before asking them to help locate my friend, but they replied that they couldn't divulge any information to me due to privacy issues. They claimed they would only cooperate with law enforcement authorities," Dave continued.

"Let me send something to Tinder to check if they could release some details to us. I'll get the relevant department to probe into this. Give me your contact number and we'll get back to you if we do hear from them, ok? This is usually not our scope of duty, but I'll make an exception to help you. At the same time, please head to the nearest precinct to file a missing person report," advised the FBI agent.

Meanwhile, Carol had been successful playing around with Google Earth. She discovered where she was located but just as she was about to check out where the police station was, Douglas appeared right behind her shoulders, "What the fuck are you doing with Google Earth?" he asked her rudely.

"I wanted to check where the location for this property is so I could feature the map next to the ad. Why?" Carol pointed at the address of a property she was planning to list on Craigslist and questioned him in a cool manner.

"You've been downgraded by Rachel to work on Craigs? Ha-ha! You must have pissed her off badly to get downgraded. Hopefully, you will get downgraded lower to just handle research. You know what they do in research? You get to do simple, boring stuff, like looking up for victims on Facebook and all those social media platforms or hacking into smartphones to pose as the owners to extort money from their contact lists. That's what research is all about!"

Carol simply ignored Douglas and let him gloat at her but was relieved she managed to escape from his suspicions.

"Carol, you're wanted," commanded Jas. "Rachel wants you in her office now."

Immediately, Carol's heart skipped a beat because she was not expecting Rachel to call her or to even have any contact with any member of the higher rank of the Syndicate just yet. However, she composed herself and headed to Rachel's office. On getting there, she knocked, but there was no answer initially; after three knocks, she was told to enter.

Rachel offered her a seat and immediately sensed the uneasiness in her.... Capitalizing on this, she spoke, "Carol, ever since you joined us, you have proven yourself well and worthy of our organization and while I rarely compliment anyone that I am proud of the person, I must say I am proud and very impressed by your performance. However, you seem to be distracted of late. Why is that so?"

Carol swallowed hard before replying, "I guess I am still suffering a little bit from the accident I had when I banged my head; guess head injury takes a longer time for full recovery."

"Alright Carol, so how about now, are you up to speed because I have got a very important assignment for you and the outcome will determine whether I will allow you to finish up with your victim or you get expelled from the Syndicate...."

With a puzzled look on her face, she asked "Expelled? How? Why?"

"Well, let's just say you won't see the sun shine ever again."

At that point, Carol became scared wondering what kind of assignment she was about to be given that such failure to succeed would warrant her death.

"Alright, as I have always given my best to the Syndicate, this will not be any different."

"Well, good because the assignment is in Germany and it's a tricky place to go for us, but since your face is relatively new, you should be able to pull it off. You know the price if you don't."

"I think it's safe to say that I am capable of rising to difficult situations because... desperate times call for desperate measures."

"No problem Carol, just pull it off and make it work. Everything you need to know is in the file and if you need anything else, talk to Jas as he will be prepping you for the trip. You leave for Flenburg, Germany tomorrow."

Carol then left Rachel's office and moved to her quarters to digest everything that just transpired between her and Rachel. She went through the file that was given to her, looking at the picture that was found in the file and all other information about him. She wasn't provided with much details of the case other than the fact that it was an operation gone wrong.

She then closed the file and slept off anticipating a new day – A day that she had little to no idea as to what may be in store for her.

THIRTY-TWO
A New Mission

6:45am

Carol was awake and stepped out from the bed to splash water on her face trying to prepare for the day's journey. She looked at herself in the mirror and seemed to see someone else. Someone from her past who looked a lot like her. She paused, poured water on her face again and checked the mirror once more and reminded herself *I'm Jamie Tan. Not Carol.* She just shrugged it off and went on to take her bath. As she was dressing up, she kept going through the file Rachel had given her and then one part struck her, the name by which she was to present herself over there. It seemed to ring another bell but still nothing concrete.

Just then Jas entered, "Looking good there missy, I think you should be able to pull this off. I believe in you and you need to believe in yourself."

"Thanks, Jas, I will never forget you no matter what. You have always been good to me and had my back during tough times."

Jas a little surprised "Is this some kind of goodbye message? You're not going to die because you will be successful. So don't even give up before trying."

Suddenly, there was the sound of a clap outside before the door opened and there stood none other than Douglas.

"Brilliant, nice encouraging talk for someone that's about to die because trust me when I tell you that this bitch is not coming back from Germany, I know what I'm saying."

Jas shot Douglas a stern look before turning back to Carol, "Just go do your thing Carol and come back with the prize."

They both left the room and entered a limousine with completely tinted bulletproof windows, but Carol was oblivious to that as she had never even seen that kind of car before. They arrived at the airstrip used for private planes. At this point, Carol began to realize the enormity of the assignment that Rachel had assigned her. Syndicate had rarely chartered the use of a private plane except for senior officials or in special cases such as this. She boarded the plane together with three ladies and three men all dressed in business suits who were en route to France because the plane was expected to transit in Paris before arriving in Flenburg.

Carol was initially scared when she saw the three men boarding the plane but was relieved when three women accompanied them looking all sexy and kinky. *Guess I will not be the only woman on the plane, Hmm'*, thought Carol before waving goodbye to Jas, who shouted to her, "Be safe missy and come back in one piece."

With that, Carol boarded the plane and for a few minutes thought about Jas; his caring nature and gentleness especially when it had anything to do with her. Jas had always shown her special attention since she got involved with the Syndicate and while there were times he would shout at her in a frustrated manner, it was all because he cared. *Maybe if things were different in another world, I could have dated Jas,* thought Carol. She smiled to herself and quickly dismissed the thought as the flight attendant announced it was time for take-off.

The plane took off, and the journey started with the men frolicking with the ladies on board while drinking and eating all at the same time. Being a private plane, there were two bedrooms, a big sitting room, and a dining area. Not long, two of the men went to the available rooms with two of the women to continue what they had started. The last man moved to the sitting room with the last girl and about 2 hours later, there was a gunshot which alarmed the flight attendants. Carol instantly ducked her head low. Suddenly the lady in the sitting room came out.

"Keep your mouth shut, comply with instructions and you will not have any problems."

The flight attendants were shaking and had their faces on the ground, it was so bad that one of them had peed on herself. Meanwhile in the other rooms, the two men had been knocked out and tied up in case they woke up at one point or another, but the drug given to them was powerful enough to make them unconscious for at least the next 12 hours.

The other two then appeared, made their way to the cockpit and instructed the pilot to make a detour instead of stopping in France but then to continue the flight to Germany or else his plane would be gunned down.

"I don't think you know who you are messing with, give up now, and you will be given a quick death," warned.

"Well, no matter," One of the ladies replied before she promptly shot his co-pilot leaving a bright smathering of blood all over the windshield. The pilot needed no other reason to comply with the instructions given to him and he opened the hatch. The ladies then left to meet the third one who was already waiting for them with 4 parachutes while Carol was left still puzzled as to what was happening. Before she could ask any questions, she was made to mount a parachute and together with the ladies they jumped down. As she went into free fall, reminiscence of her past came flashing back as she recalled her first experience sky diving during her trip in Australia. Tears started flowing down her cheeks as she saw her twins running towards her the minute she landed safely after her skydiving adventure. She was certain she had to find a way to escape from this entire saga and reunite with her boys.

Thirty minutes later, they were on the ground in a remote village near Marseille, France.

They entered an old house that looked tattered and abandoned and after twenty minutes inside the house, Carol, dumbfounded and deeply shaken, opened her mouth and asked, "Please what are we doing here? What have I even done wrong that you had to abduct me?"

One of the ladies smiled and said, "You just watch baby girl. You will understand soon."

Just then one of them pressed a button, and a latch opened revealing a large base of operations which was well-lit with people working and interacting, some of them seemed to have previously been involved in combat training. She kept moving with the ladies and was in awe of the whole place, especially the high level of technology on display.

She was given a room to freshen up and change into new clothes. When she was through, she was ushered into a large office to which sat a blonde lady of about 5'9" with an athletic and sexy body. When Carol entered, the lady lifted her face from the laptop she was working on and welcomed her, "Well, I know you have a lot of questions on your mind, but trust me when I tell you that all will be answered and explained in due time. So why not relax, make yourself at home and then tomorrow morning we will talk. I am Evelyn, by the way."

Reluctantly, Carol replied, "Alright, thanks."

The following morning, Carol woke up and for the first time in a while, she took her time in the bathroom to have her bath, soaking in the water while enjoying the ambience as well as the tranquility around her. While she was dressing up, someone came up to her room to inform her that breakfast was ready. Five minutes later Carol was out of her room having her breakfast, and afterwards, she was ushered into Evelyn's office. For a moment, Carol could do nothing but admire her; her tenacity and her coordination of such an organization like this, which comprised mainly of women. On top of that, she was beautiful, bold and strong. She was brought out of her reverie when she heard "Welcome Carol, hope you slept well?"

"Hmm, yes I did; been a while since I slept that peacefully."

"Well, good to know. So, why don't you take a seat and let's get down to business so we can both help each other out."

Carol, who knew better than to start asking unnecessary questions simply, nodded her head and sat down.

"Now," Evelyn began, "I know you are part of a group called the Syndicate which is an astute criminal organization that is adept at scamming people and has ties with terrorist groups. I understand you were coerced into joining the group, even though you seem to have gotten excellent at your job to be sent out into the field". Evelyn allowed what she just said to sink into Carol and patiently allowed her to digest it. True enough, Carol had a puzzled look on her face. On noticing this, Evelyn continued, "Now, I am sure you're wondering how is it that I know so much about the Syndicate and you in particular. Well. I used to be part of the Syndicate until they killed someone I cared about."

THIRTY-THREE
Is this Syndicate's Alliance?

Evelyn started relaying her side of the story which had happened five years ago in Houston, Texas.

"Hey Evelyn, just wait for it; at least it's meant for you."

"You know I don't like to be kept waiting, and I don't do too well with surprises."

"Well, it's me baby, and you are gonna have to like it, and trust me when you see it you will love it! It's all gonna be worth it."

Evelyn's boyfriend, Kevin, who was about to be her fiancé led her to a room not knowing what to expect, but he was almost sweating from anticipation. Eventually, the blindfold was lifted, and Evelyn was speechless because she was in a well-lit room decorated with flowers, and enclosed in sweet aroma. The table was set, and the food appeared to be her favorite - Chinese food. She was flushed all over with tear drops gathering on her eyelids, and all she could do was cover her face with her two hands and just hug Kevin.

"I love you, baby, you're the best thing that has ever happened to me and thanks for accepting me the way I am."

"Well, the feeling's mutual, dearie, I really love you too and I can give my life for you because you're worth everything I have including my life."

"Com'on Kevin, that's a little too exaggerating don't you think?"

"Nothing is too small or too much for you, Angel."

So the both of them sat down to eat gazing at each other's faces, smiling. Evelyn couldn't help but admire Kevin, this handsome devil of hers. He was over six feet tall with a chiseled face, well-built body and seemingly perfect eyes. He was any woman's dream and no matter how angry or stressed from work he was, he always treated her gently, like a queen. He worked at a reputable law firm just outside of Houston and was a good lawyer. While he wore a different persona when attending to cases and clients, he never brought work with him when he was with Evelyn.... She was his muse. She meant everything to him, and he could give his life for her. Kevin was indeed a protector. He held a black belt in Judo and was also well trained in jujitsu because he was taken in at a young age by a martial artist after the death of his parents. He was simply a product of life's toughness and tenacity. Women flocked around him, but he never gave them attention until he met Evelyn. She was just irresistible and since then, there had been no turning back.

When they finished eating, Kevin moved closer to her, touching her ears as he produced a rose from behind his back. He carefully gave her the stem before bringing his other hand forward and opening his palm to reveal two diamond earrings.

"Wow, Kevin, you're simply amazing, and I must say that you are my life."

Kevin just smiled, and while she was still in awe of the earrings and flower, he brought out a small box and got down on his knees, "Evelyn Lane, ever since you have been in my life, I have never had a moment of sadness because even in my lowest moments, you were there to pull me up and give me reason to continue moving forward. So darling, will you make me a happy man and marry me?"

If Evelyn was initially speechless, now she was stunned, but she still managed to maintain her composure.

"Yes I will, and I love you with all my heart, Kevin."

"Well, I don't love you that much," Kevin teased her with a smile on his face. Evelyn hit him playfully and then he carried her into the bedroom.

A week later on a Saturday morning, Kevin was working on his laptop while Evelyn was sleeping, suddenly there came a beeping light on Evelyn's laptop which Kevin was reluctant to check at first, but as it kept flashing continuously, he decided to check it out and what he found surprised him. Evelyn had been asked to transfer a ridiculous amount of money to one of the groups her organization was affiliated with.

Now, Kevin was not entirely convinced about Evelyn's line of work when she told him she was working for an investment firm which he had not heard about. He eventually made his findings and located the investment office but his gut still told him something wasn't right, but since he couldn't get anything else, he let it slide. However, this brought back that gut feeling again and being a lawyer, he decided to probe further. Luckily for him, he knew his way with the computer, and he began to see the activities of the organization his fiancé was working with.

He made a mental note of the information he collected which he thought could possibly be useful to him and closed the laptop when he noticed Evelyn stirring in her sleep. In the morning, he dressed up for work and kissed her goodbye. The minute he got into his car, he called his Dad, the martial art expert who adopted him and explained what he had found, his dad then told him to visit that evening after work to discuss everything in person.

Later that evening Kevin met up with his father as planned.

"Evening son, have you forgotten your dad now that there is your career and a woman?" his dad asked.

"No dad, you know how it is, it's a fast world and almost a rat race with little or no time for other things, and I am really sorry."

"No problem son, at least you're here. So how is your woman?"

"She is fine Dad and like you know, she's my reason for being here this evening."

So father and son sat down to discuss the situation and the next line of action.

About a week later Evelyn was at a meeting where they were discussing the progress of the organization and the fact that they had discovered someone sniffing around. CCTV footage was then played showing a man about six feet two with a well-built and athletic body trying to extract some information from a laptop, a minute after, the camera went blank which might have been knocked out by the man's accomplice.

The boss then spoke with a loud and clear voice of a woman, "We need to find the son of a bitch that did this and send him straight to hell." There was a murmur of agreement from the people seated, but one was deep in thought. The boss noticed this and addressed her, "You got something on your mind, Evelyn?"

"Well, Rachel, nobody knows about what we do here except those of us in this room. So it has to be that someone among us must have opened an avenue for that to happen and this person, when caught, should be dealt with along with the perpetrator. But since we do not murder people, how then will we deal with them?"

"You have raised a good point Evelyn, but you leave that to me, I will take care of that issue. You just locate the mole and the thief and bring them to me." With that, they all dispersed and went about their duties.

Two weeks later at the next meeting, there was good news and bad to report as Rachel commenced the meeting, "Well, after two weeks of intensive search, we finally found both the mole and the thief, and you will not be expecting who might be the culprit." Then a young man by the name of Douglas stood up and played a video on the large screen in front of them showing Kevin breaking into the organization's safe after neutralizing the guards. Kevin was aware of the cameras in that room but what he overlooked was a hidden camera and a tracker on the safe such that a touch on it will alert Douglas. So once the tracker was triggered, the organization would be prompted of an intruder and they would have discovered everything about the latter through facial recognition. That was why they allowed him to escape with the intention to revenge on him at a later time when he least expected. Now Evelyn was sweating not because she was scared of what will be done to her but she feared for Kevin's life. Douglas then spoke, "Now, to the mole that helped the thief or should I say the thief's lover, chill out for the next footage...", he played another video featuring a series of pictures of Evelyn and Kevin together.

There was now murmuring in the meeting room, and all eyes were fixed on Evelyn, "You bitch, traitor, you're going to burn. Just wait until Amir Sayed gets a hold of you." These were the words echoing in the room until they heard Rachel raising her voice.

"Silence! Everyone but Jas and Evelyn, leave the room."

Everyone left, leaving just the three of them in the room. "I am disappointed in you, Evelyn but I am curious, what do you have to say for yourself?"

"There's nothing I can say that will justify or change your mind about what happened, so you might as well bring the heat."

Rachel smiled, "Well I knew you were tough and strong, but I never figured you were plain foolish. When we are through with your thief of a boyfriend, you will be sorry that you ever crossed the line."

Evelyn was then hauled by Jas into a room used for holding members who crossed the organization. All her belongings were confiscated from her, in fact, she was almost stripped, but then Rachel changed her mind at the last minute.

Later that evening, Kevin got home from work and realized Evelyn wasn't around. He dialed her number but couldn't get through to her. He began to get that gut feeling again that something was wrong. He sensed that maybe they were on to her, but he knew he couldn't do anything at that moment. After hours of walking around and pacing trying to find a solution, he got a text on his phone that read, *"Please leave. They are coming for you, and they are going to burn you alive. Love E."*

Kevin knew at once that it was Evelyn, but she definitely had been apprehended and was about to be punished for his sins. He immediately called his Dad to explain the situation to him and the latter adviced him to go over as he had a plan in mind. The next evening, Amir Sayed's men went to Kevin's house, entered stealthily and saw Kevin sleeping. They poured gasoline around the house and blew up the house with him sleeping in it.

The next day, they hauled Evelyn to Kevin's house to look at the fate of her lover to get a feel of what would happen to people that crossed the organization. She broke down in tears and after five minutes, she stopped crying braced herself and entered the car. She was driven back to the Syndicate and then thrown back in the room she was being held pending the Syndicate's final decision of her fate.

Three weeks on and Evelyn was still being held as a prisoner. She was being fed like a pig and only allowed to have her bath once a week. Unknown to them, she had been perfecting her plan of getting back at the Syndicate for destroying her 'happiness', after killing Kevin. She had been talking with one of the guards whom she had always been good to and that one had been helping her to set combustible materials at strategic places in the building which Syndicate operated. When she was given a usual chance of taking her bath the last week, the perfect time had come. With the help of that guard, she managed to set an explosion at one end of the building where she was, and the fire kept spreading causing panic and a mess among members of the Syndicate. Nobody could bother about anyone else, even Douglas and Jas had to run for their lives while trying to protect Rachel. Evelyn made the complete accident seemed like the cause of the fire was due to a faulty wire in the building's electrical system which they had not gotten down to fixing due to distractions coming from Evelyn's case. Just then they remembered her, "Douglas, how about Evelyn, guess she must have been burnt in the fire."

"Well guess she got what she deserved."

"Come on Doug, she's still one of us," said Jas.

"Well not in my good books Jas. You always have a soft spot for blondes, particularly this one so don't even get me started."

"It's alright boys, let's just get out of here," and with that, they left and drove away.

Moments later, the guard that helped Evelyn went on to open a sewer outlet and out came to a lady covered with soot from the burning flames.

"For a moment I thought you were gone."

"Thanks but you should know it will take more than this fire to take me out."

"I know, but let's get out of here."

THIRTY-FOUR
Back to the present day

Back at Syndicate's headquarters...

"What in the world happened to Carol?" beamed Rachel, "Could she have pulled this all by herself? She rarely has contact with the outside world except for the clients she had to deal with or could any of them have helped her?" continued Rachel.

"Well, as much as I do not like her, I am not so sure she could have pulled this off and with the way the whole scene was described by the flight attendant, it seemed very well choreographed even for law enforcement agencies," Douglas replied.

"So are you saying that we should rule out law enforcement agencies from this operation? I mean who could have known that itinerary?" asked Rachel.

"I don't really have an answer to that right now, but I think we still have those hidden cameras on the plane. I will check out the footage once the mess in the plane has been cleaned up and the bodies have been taken care of," replied Douglas.

Rachel nodded and said: "Send me updates on anything you find.”

“Sure thing Rach."

Meanwhile in Marseille, France...
"See Carol, I know everything there is to know about you including your background and I can provide you with everything you need to know as long as you help us take down Syndicate starting with ensuring Bertrand is recaptured after the mission given to you by Rachel," said Evelyn.

“Well about the whole memory thing, it's all still fuzzy, and I would really like to know more about my past and what the Syndicate has been keeping from me.” Jamie decided to keep her true identity for now and resume the name Carol as she felt there wasn't need to alert anyone for now since she had totally lost the trust of everybody around her.

"Good then I guess we have a deal. Now we're going to run through the plan with you so that we can both get what we want which is to bring Syndicate to its knees."

Just as Carol was about to leave, Evelyn tapped her head and said, "That reminds me, Carol, let me show you a little bit of how we work.”

Just then the three ladies that were on board the plane with Carol appeared, but they looked different which left Carol stunned, "You were a brunette with a round face.... And you...you looked Middle Eastern... Wait... Wow, you all did a great job disguising yourselves as you carried out your operations."

"Yeah that's right and the plane you were on had hidden cameras so we had to conceal our true identities but don't worry we got you covered."

With a puzzled look on her face, Carol inquired, "Got me covered? How?"

"You don't have to worry about that, just leave that to us."

"Guess I will stop asking questions then."

The ladies stepped out of the room leaving just Evelyn and Carol.

*****

Douglas was busy with the video footage recovered from the plane and was going over it when he got to a point where the ladies on capturing who they wanted spoke, "You have something that belongs to Amir, and he is coming for his debt. You know he always collects."

Immediately, Douglas shuddered in his seat, and the other tech guys could not help but notice the change in his reaction; Douglas was a fearless guy who rarely got scared so for him to react that way, meant a lot and he had every right to be fearful.

Amir Sayed was not a man to be messed with; he was probably the most ruthless man to have emerged from the world of terrorism leaving a trail of death and destruction in his wake. There was a time a group of people promised him some state-of-the-art weapons to further his operations but something happened, and they failed to deliver as planned. When he realized that, he killed every one of them and all those connected to them including family and friends leaving his calling card "Amir always collects." It was his ruthlessness that endeared him to Syndicate and then began to use his services up until the point they employed him to settle scores with Evelyn's boyfriend, Kevin, which they were not able to complete payment for him since they had to flee from Texas. That was where they lost connection and Amir had been looking for an opportunity to get back at them to exert his revenge. One peculiar thing about Amir Sayed was his stealth in operations because his enemies never see him coming- this was the part that scared Douglas. Yes, he was brave, but he was not ready to die some foolish death over circumstantial events and immediately he went to Rachel's office.

Douglas rushed to Rachel's office and barged in without knocking; while Rachel was not a persistent advocate of protocols, she still preferred when someone knocked before entering her office no matter the person's position in the organization. Hence when Douglas entered without knocking, she frowned and was about to curse at him when she looked up and observed his facial expression which told her something was wrong, "What's wrong Doug? Is everything alright? What did you discover?" Rachel blurted out all the questions in quick successions.

"It's Amir Sayed," Douglas replied without mincing his words.

Instantly, Rachel's face turned pale, and the hair on her skin stood. The name sent a chill down her spine and for a moment, she became speechless. Raising her head from her hands, she looked at Douglas and asked "What do we do? We all know how Amir Sayed operates. You never see him coming until he is right behind you."

"Well, for now, I don't know. All I can say is I do not want to die a horrible death and definitely not in the hands of that monster. I'd rather kill myself than let that bastard touch me."

"I guess we are doomed, aren't we? I knew that incident five years ago was going to come back to haunt us which was why I tried to get across to him but unfortunately, he only works through an intermediary which we lost after that same incident. Only God knows what Carol is going through, and Bertrand is still in the custody of the authority; things haven't been this bad since Evelyn decided to sell us out."

Douglas replied and said: "Let's forget about all of them for now. We need to find a way to reach Amir or better still, locate Carol since she holds the keys to getting Bertrand free and after that, we can then find a way to deal with Amir."

"You've got a point there. Why not get to tracing her again if the tracker will respond."

"Alright then, no problem."

THIRTY-FIVE
Portugal

"I hope you have it figured out now, and you understand what you're expected to do right?" Evelyn asked. Carol nodded and collected the device given to her by Evelyn. After giving her the mass storage device that contained all the information she might need, she was then directed to the tech department where she was given another device- a communication device that was encrypted and undetectable.

"You simply need to be able to hide this long enough for you to use it and communicate with us so we can track your progress and ascertain your location," the tech man said, handing her the device.

"Alright, I will keep that in mind," replied Carol.

She was directed to a room where she was slightly beaten just to give an impression of someone that was kidnapped. She was then driven to an airstrip in Paris where she was put on a plane that would drop her somewhere near Portugal. It was there that the tracker was turned back on, and that was when the Syndicate could ascertain her location. She then booked the next available flight to Germany which was slated for the next day.

Later that day, she booked a room in a hotel to settle in. She decided to get a payphone and contacted David, who picked when the phone barely made its first ring.

"Hello, David, this is Jamie."

"God, where have you been? I have been frantically trying to get to you, but I have largely met dead ends."

"It's a long story. I was almost caught with you which was when they changed my duties and gave me something else to do. Then they gave me an assignment to rescue one of their agents in Germany."

"So what, are you in Germany right now?"

"Well, not exactly."

"Okay, where are you then?"

"Right now, I am in Portugal and have just checked into a hotel as I wait for the flight to Germany that will happen tomorrow."

"Hope you're safe, sweet."

"Yes I am, at least at the moment, but I don't know what will happen tomorrow."

"Don't say that. You will get through this and come back to me alive."

"I hope so Dave, I really do. Let me get back to preparing for tomorrow before they get smart and start tracing this call."

"I've got the German inspector, Ms. Agneta Otto's contact with me. I went into the email account you gave me access to after the incident. Do you want me to get a hold of her?" And *beep* went the tone of the phone.

Then Carol made another call this time to the Syndicate, which was picked up by Rachel. "Hello, this is Carol, I hope you have an idea of what has been going on. I was almost killed for you."

Rachel feigning ignorance said, "I am so sorry Carol, but I am glad to hear you're alive. I wish it could have been avoided but where were you taken?" As Rachel was talking to Carol, she signaled for Douglas through the window from her office to get him to track the call from Carol.

"I don't know, but all I know is I was dropped off in Portugal, and I am here right now, but I have booked the next flight to Germany which leaves tomorrow."

"Wow, I never knew you had emergency cash on you."

"You gave me a credit card to use in case of an emergency, and that was what I used."

"Oh, yeah that's true, but we lost track of you, any idea how that happened??"

"Well that I have no idea, but I am definitely going to give my best in getting this assignment done and show you my worth once again, then maybe, just maybe you will learn to trust me again."

"Alright, you finish the assignment and come home, then we shall talk about trust." So she dropped the call and just then Douglas entered the office and said, "The bitch is in Portugal, and I think she engineered this. But there wasn't enough time to track her exact location."

She simply smiled and said, "Calm yourself, I know, she just called and reassured me of her commitment to the assignment. So just keep tracking her."

With a puzzled look, Douglas grudgingly replied, "Okay then, guess I will keep tabs on her."

"Do that then," commanded Rachel.

The next morning Carol got dressed and prepared for her flight. She went to the airport and was checked in, silently hoping and praying there was not going to be another traumatic incident on this particular flight. True to it, she got to Germany, and she checked into a hotel room already booked for her by the Syndicate in Frankfurt. There she was met by one of their agents who showed her what she had to do and reminded her of what was at stake. She then went over the file handed to her and studied it trying to come up with the line to pitch to the authorities. It wasn't an easy job, but she was confident of pulling it through. She lay on her bed lost in thought and was tempted to pick up the phone to call David again, but she knew better. *Let me not put myself in further trouble or raise more suspicions. Time to get some food and sleep to prepare for tomorrow.*

She ordered room service as she wanted to keep a low profile as much as she could before the mission the next day. She examined the storage device given to her by Evelyn. Despite her urge to get a laptop somewhere and take a quick preview of the information it might have contained about her and her old life, she knew that she could not take the risk. She was also now paranoid and aware of the Syndicate's constant watch and having just promised Rachel that she was going to win her trust back via the completion of this assignment, she was so not ready to put herself under unnecessary suspicion.

THIRTY-SIX
Rising up to the Challenge

At approximately 8:00am in the morning, Carol was ready with her files and outfit; looking as though she was heading for an important company board meeting. As she waited for her ride, she was accompanied by one of Syndicate's agent that had flown in to help her with the case and she suspected was also there to ensure she didn't sell them out. No party was willing to take any chances especially the Syndicate not with the arrival of Amir Sayed in the equation.

By 8:30am, Carol's ride arrived, and there was a knock on the door to which she responded, "Come in, the door is open."

The door opened and in stepped a six-foot blonde-haired fierce-looking man.

"You should be Carol right?" without waiting for a reply from Carol, he continued, "Well let's get going then."

"And you are?" asked Carol.

"Ivan."

His thick Russian accent could not be hidden in his attempt to sound like a gentleman while trying hard to converse in English as Carol couldn't help but noticed. She made up her mind to be as smart as possible to get this job done perfectly because the man seemed like someone who would not hesitate to put a bullet in her brain if she tried anything funny.

She simply picked the briefcase containing her files and meekly followed the 'gentleman' to the car. After driving for about 30 minutes, they got to the Frankfurt office where Bertrand was being held.

They entered the office and were being checked, "Carol Yang, right?"

"Yes, that's right."

"So what's in the briefcase?"

"Just files concerning my client's case."

"And who's your tough-looking friend?"

Just then, the man with Carol wanted to step forward, but she pulled him to the side and said, "Calm down, let's not blow this."

"Fine, take this device, as it allows us to keep in touch and I don't need to tell you what will happen if you try anything funny."

With that, Carol walked back to the checkpoint and by then, Inspector Agnetha Otto was there discussing with the security, "Hello, what are you doing here?" The inspector asked Carol. "And please hand me your identity."

Carol handed over her documents and identified herself.

"I'm here to bail my client out."

"Well, what's the name of your client?"

"That will be Bertrand whom you have been holding for the past two weeks."

With a puzzled look, she asked, "So how are you related to Bertrand? You know he's committed a criminal offence, don't you?"

"I'm his legal representative. My client works for a marriage counselling agency, you have our employee on a charge that's baseless, and I am here to bail him out," Carol replied, aware that Ivan, the Russian gentleman was monitoring and listening to her conversations while waiting outside for her.

"Do you have any local documents to prove your professional status here in Germany?"

Carol passed her all the necessary documents to prove she had the legal rights to represent Bertrand in Germany.

Inspector Otto scrutinized the documents in detail and looked up at Carol, "Well right this way then, I will take you to him."

On realizing that they were out of the radar from Ivan's staring eyes, Carol slipped a note into Inspector Otto's hands which she quickly read and folded to place it into her pocket. She showed Carol the holding room where Bertrand was sitting.

"Can I get some privacy with my client? You know, Lawyer-client privilege." Carol asked.

Inspector Otto turned to leave, before looking back, "The cameras has been turned off as well."

"Well, thanks that will be appreciated."

Carol entered the room and introduced herself to Bertrand, who didn't look like he cared much for introduction.

"Guess you're here to get me out right? Because I have been here far too long."

Carol simply shrugged, "Well I am, but you will have to trust me."

"I don't know who the fuck you are, never seen you before, and you expect me to trust you, just like that?"

"I am appointed as your attorney, and I should be the one asking questions, but you sure got a lot of questions in that thick head of yours. Wait, what's the problem? Abandoned as a kid, no one wanted to take you in and those that did just treated you like an animal…"

Carol waited to see how he would react upon receiving her comments and realized she had struck a nerve.

"So eventually you decided to be on the streets and fend for yourself rather than be given the most inhumane treatment in someone else's house. That was until you met the Dominos' who took you in and treated you like family, taught you the family trade and since then, you have never looked back, am I right?" she continued.

Bertrand was silent for a moment trying to digest what had just been said. The Dominos' were a part of his life that nobody knew about except for Rachel and her father but if this person was from Rachel, how the hell did she take so long to come to his rescue?

"Fine, since you know so much about me, who sent you and whose interest do you represent?"

Carol smiled and replied him, "I am from the Scorpion, and I was told to bring home the Viper at all costs."

Immediately, Bertrand's eyes lit up, and he smiled.

"She sent you directly didn't she? I thought maybe she had abandoned me just like everyone else in my life did. Guess I was wrong."

"Well, a lot is going on right now that I am not in a position to tell you. The best person you'd want to ask is Rachel. My priority is to get you out of here."

"And how do you intend to do that?"

"Well, why don't you leave that to me? Just let me work my magic."

Meanwhile, Inspector Otto was back at her desk and decided to check the content of the note she received earlier from Carol.

"I'm not sure if you know of an Inspector Agnetha Otto from Flensburg. She has my case in file. I'm Jamie Tan from Canada, who had lodged a complaint with the German authorities about a year back. I'm currently held hostage by the Syndicate. Please make it possible for him to be released because that way, you

will get everything you need to arrest him and his cohorts. And you might want to find a way to track him down as he could lead you to the rest of the perpetrators. There's a plan in place."

What baffled her was the persona of the woman that gave her the note; she was definitely a far cry from the woman that kept seeking her help frantically a few months ago to be saved from scammers. *Guess everyone has a bit of badass in them, just need to be in a situation to trigger it,* she thought to herself.

"You know you have no grounds to hold my client this long right, and we could sue you for this."

"Well, we have ground because he claimed that he needed some money for business from a citizen of ours and we cannot find any record of that business anywhere. More so he had pretended to be a woman." Inspector Otto replied in fluent English with traces of German accent.

"Well, here's a record of the business showing its existence, how this loan he was looking to obtain will get the business back on track and allow him to make more profit." She then gave the inspector a file containing a record of the business and true to it, it proved there weren't any grounds to detain Bertrand any longer.

With a puzzled look, she asked, "How come we were not able to find it?"

"Well, it's from Czech Republic, and you are not exactly expected to list all your business records unless you're trying to obtain a large amount of money as a loan from the bank."

"Okay fine, how do you explain the whole woman disguise and pretense?"

"That has little or no ground, and I can be whoever I choose to be, it's my choice and last I checked as citizens, we still have that right."

Feeling defeated, Inspector Otto smiled and shrugged, "Fine have it your way; just sign these papers and your client is free to go."

Carol signed the papers, got Bertrand freed and they went out to meet Ivan, who was waiting for them in front of the car. Ivan, who had been listening to the conversation the whole time, couldn't help but be impressed by this confident woman who had just pulled off an amazing job. That meant something because Ivan was a difficult man to make an impression on and Carol did it without even trying to.

"Guess I owe you my life then, sorry I doubted you."

Carol simply smiled and told him, "No worries, I am glad to be of help. Now I see why Rachel has gone to all this length to get you out."

Carol knew Bertrand had a part in collecting the money she had been scammed off and that she had him arrested the first time in Flensburg when she lodged a report to the authorities back in April 2015. As much as she wanted to ask him about the incident in Flensburg, she knew she had to hold back and not reveal to Syndicate that she was gradually regaining her memory.

From there, they had a silent ride to their hotel as they went on to prepare for the next available flight to return to the US.

THIRTY-SEVEN
Homecoming King

Three days later, Bertrand and Carol arrived back in North Carolina; the delay was due to a heavy storm that started the day of Bertrand's release and continued to the next day. They got to Syndicate's office and Rachel personally came out to meet them. Carol had never seen Rachel that excited about something or someone. And rightly so because Bertrand was like a brother to Rachel, and they both treasured one another; in another lifetime or line of work, if no one knew how they were related, they could have passed on as a married couple, but as it was, they were both close but more so in a brother-sister relationship.
She hugged Bertrand before leading him back inside.

"Carol, please meet me in my office in the next hour for a full report," she said over her shoulder as she walked away.

"Yes, ma'am," Carol replied.

Carol was then checked and declared free to go to her room; Douglas and Jas were also there, and while Jas also welcomed Bertrand with some level of excitement, Douglas was unmoved which was not surprising as he had always only tolerated Bertrand because he was so close to the Domino family. He was also jealous of him because he wanted Rachel to himself and he felt it was unfair that Bertrand was always her favourite. In fact, he was secretly gloating when they discovered Bertrand had gotten caught by the authorities. The only reason he decided to trace Carol was to protect his own head coupled with the fact that he'd never liked her, and was hoping trouble would befall her.

"I trust they had nothing on you right?" asked Rachel.

"No, they didn't though I almost gave in when I saw no help whatsoever from you thinking maybe you had abandoned me."

"And why would I do that? You are the closest thing to family that I have got left, and I will never abandon you, especially not after everything that we have been through."

"Well, I trust you won't and that lady you sent, pulled off a terrific job."

"Well, I left her with little or no choice; either she successfully gets you out, or she dies. That was the deal, and I guess she still values her life, so she just had to get it done."

"Wow, amazing but then she mentioned that some unforeseen events came up which made the 'cavalry' arrive late."

"Yes Bertrand, the plane she was on was attacked, and she herself was captured and went missing for a week."

"What?? Who could have done that and are you sure she wasn't the one that pulled it off considering you threatened her?"

"Now, for starters, she had a day's notice about the assignment and the plane was a private chartered plane with hidden cameras, after careful review of the video feed which was partly damaged thanks to the crash, we discovered it was Amir Sayed."

On hearing that name, Bertrand's jaw dropped but then immediately, he composed himself and said, "Now I understand but then what have you done about it so far?"

"Hmmmm, nothing exactly because we have been trying to figure out a way to get you released after which we can use some of your expertise to figure out a way to tackle this problem and deal with him for good. Now that you are released, well maybe Sayed can be taken care of."

"Alright, let me go through that feed again and see if I can pick up one or two things from there."

"No problem, fix yourself up with food and then start work."

"Sure thing Rach, I really miss you dishing out instructions trying to take care of me."

"Maybe, you need to come home more often and not only when there are meetings."

Bertrand simply smiled and walked away. He met Carol on the way and thanked her once again for her efforts in getting him released.

Carol went straight to Rachel's office and knocked, "Come on in," came Rachel's voice from the other side.

She opened the door and entered.

"Welcome, I really want to thank you for all your efforts to get my brother released. It really means a lot to me and because of that I will reinstate you, and you can start raking in more clients for us."

Carol took a deep breath "But..."

"Yes, you're right, there's a but, however, it's not difficult. I just need you to try and remember anything you can about where you were taken to."

"Alright, I know we jumped off the plane around Belgium, and we drove for some time before getting out in a village that seemed deserted. We went in deeper and, I was taken to a villa where I was then thrown into a room, I was blindfolded throughout the drive."

"Well, thanks, Carol, this should help us to find out Sayed's exact location and make him pay for what he did to you. I will give you your phone back, and you can finish up with your client Rob, that's his name right?"

"Yes, I believe so, but I don't know if he is still interested."

"Well, interested or not, I am pulling you off listing duties on Craigs and back to your original post; more so there is still a lot of dumb asses out there ready to give beautiful women their money, so get to work."

"No problem, as you wish ma'am."

Carol walked out of Rachel's office and was given back her phone. Instead of contacting Rob immediately, she decided against it and decided to modify her profile to get new clients but this time, she had something else in mind. She knew she had to be careful and smart about her next move else it might mean the end of her.

David meanwhile was still trying to reach out to Jamie but to no avail. He was hoping to find out if she was back from Germany as he had been thinking about what was going to be his next step. Not long after, he got a call. He picked up immediately.

"Hello?"

No reply for about a minute and just as he was about to cut the call out of anger he heard a voice at the other end, one he couldn't miss, "Hello David it's me."

"Jamie are you back? Hope you're safe?"

"Yes I am, and now I will be using my own personal phone which I got from my little trip to Germany."

"Are you alone? Is that not a bit risky, I mean what if you are caught with using it? I won't forgive myself if anything happens to you."

"Don't worry, I have got my allies now, and the phone is encrypted, it cannot be tracked, and my journey has been a sort of an epiphany so I am a little more paranoid than before and more careful."

"Alright then, I trust you, sweet, but please for my sake be very careful."

"Sure, contact you-know-who in Germany. Talk to you later."

With that, Carol cut the call and set about to her work but the timer was set, and the race was on to bringing down the Syndicate.

THIRTY-EIGHT
The Reckoning

Life was back to normal routine at the Syndicate with little news to tell. Bertrand returned to Prague, Jas still had a soft spot for Carol and Douglas still kept to himself while at the same time unwavering in his desire to trust or like Carol. In fact, he wished she had not been able to rescue Bertrand so that he would be able to get the chance to have Rachel's attention and probably win her over. He was sitting in his cubicle one day thinking, *Can't I just get out of this hellhole right now and give this guy what he wants so he can let me be, and I can just start a new life?*

As if in response to that thought, there was a beep on the device in his hand and he immediately went to the restroom where there were no surveillance devices like cameras or audio device pickers and accepted the call.

"Hello?"

"Listen, Doug," came the distorted voice which was typical of Amir Sayed when talking to people that he had assignments for.

"Yes, I am listening," Doug began, with a little fear detectable in his voice.

Satisfied, the distorted voice kept speaking, "You have between 7-10 days to get more funds across to me and provide me your accurate location or you will be made to wish you were dead, got it?"

"Yes, I do, and I am working on it, just please don't kill me. I really need to get out of here and enjoy my life. You know, use my brain for something better."

"Well, that's none of my business, see all I am concerned about is my money that wasn't paid to me five years ago, and once you help me get that, you will have everything you need and whatever you do afterwards with your life is none of my business as long as you don't cross my path again."

"As you wish, I better get back to work then."

Douglas then walked out of the restroom and met Carol on the way who smiled and greeted him and for the first time, he actually acknowledged and greeted her back. This shocked Carol, rather than be impressed, she got a bad feeling in her gut that something was not right with him, but since she had made it her new business to stay out of other people's businesses, she simply shook it off and continued to make her way to the restroom.

Douglas got back to his station and began to strategize on how he was going to get the funds across while not compromising with the new identity he had created for himself. He then cast his mind back to about 2 months ago when it all began. He'd gone out for his regular walk which was one privilege Rachel gave him since he rarely talked to anyone. That was when a van suddenly stopped in front of him and before he knew what had happened, he was blindfolded and thrown into it. He was driven to an unknown storage warehouse, but he didn't know until he got down and heard the way sounds were echoing and bouncing off walls.

He was seated on a chair and left alone for about a few minutes before someone came out and spoke, "Welcome, surprised to be here right, well we just need a tiny little bit of your help. See, your people owe me some money for a previous job I did, and I am back to collect."

Immediately when Douglas heard the last part of that statement, he started to struggle to get out of his bonds but to no avail.

"No, no listen, Amir, we didn't mean to, but our office got burned down, and we had to relocate. In fact, we tried to reach out to you but to no avail." Douglas tried to clarify.

He was replied to with a hysterical laugh, "Well, guess again cockroach because you're doomed, and unless you help me get what I want, you are going down with your organization. As a matter of fact, how about I end your miserable life right now?"

The next sound Douglas heard was that of a gun being cocked.

"Alright, fine you win. I will do whatever you want, but I need something in return."

"Well, ask then."

"I will like a new passport with a change of identity, and I get to start afresh because I intend to do more for myself than just serve the Syndicate all my life."

There was a loud burst of laughter followed by, "Alright guess you got yourself a deal then. Let's shake on it, shall we?"

As Douglas stretched out his hand to shake the other man's hand, he just felt a surge of electricity run through him, and he shook furiously on the seat he was tied to.

"Well Douglas, that's my assurance, injected and sealed, awaiting for your delivery. And in case you decide to double cross me, I will take you out with the simple push of a button no matter where you are. You will just feel your body disintegrated and scatter within 2 minutes, so think it through before you make your next foolish move."

It was at that point that a familiar voice seemed to wake him up from his reverie;

"Rachel needs your attention in her office," said a young lady of about 18 years of age.

Douglas picked himself up and went straight to Rachel's office to figure out why he was suddenly called upon and when he got there, what he saw made him stare in horror and disbelief. Rachel's computer system was completely blown to bits. The only reason she wasn't dead was because the person who sent the message that crashed her laptop didn't want her dead. Douglas knew he had better get his butt moving with the assignment from Amir Sayed or he was going to be done for, and there would be little or no day-dreaming of a better life ever again.

Rachel explained everything to him and without uttering a word, he carried the crashed laptop to try to salvage whatever was left from the damage. At the same time, he went on to prepare a new one for her to use.

At that moment, she knew she had to just go for a walk to calm her nerves after downing a whole bottle of whiskey; she was not one who'd turned to alcohol as an escape but at this point she needed something strong to make sense of whatever that have been going on with the Syndicate while trying to maintain her composure, with strong hope that she could ride the storm and come out on top.

THIRTY-NINE
Back In The Saddle

Carol was seated in her room checking and phishing profiles from social media sites, trying to look for new clients for Syndicate. While she had it in mind to plot a revenge mission, she couldn't afford to raise suspicions by failing to bring in revenues which led her to make some changes to her online profile. She kept searching and muttering to herself 'No, no, no not this one' all the while swiping through each potential client until she got to one that fit the profile. This time, she was as careful about those she picked as clients as she was aware that the best targets were those perceived to be wealthy perverts, gullible in reasoning, yet vulnerable and desperate. After several attempts, she found no one that fit the bill, she decided to go ahead and check out other things on the Internet like the latest fashion trends, music and general news around the world. She was checking through looking at various ladies displaying their hair and clothes and she couldn't help but wonder what it would feel like to be a model and just have people appreciate her beauty as it should be and get paid for it rather than have to pretend about who she was and go on swindling people out of their money. *But if wishes were horses beggars would ride, right?* While she was doing this, she examined the mass storage device that Evelyn had handed over to her which contained everything she needed to know about herself. *What if I check it, and I get disappointed by what I find? Or I get caught checking it? That will ruin everything.... No, it's not going to happen because now I am smarter and better at what I do but at the same time I still have to be careful.*

Just as these thoughts were going through her mind, Jas came in and quickly she hid the device pretending she didn't know he was there.

"Hello, earth to Carol" Jas shouted as he waved his hand at her.

Finally, she seemed to come back to life from her reverie.

"Damn girl! Where have you been? Where did you go?"

"Sorry, was caught up in the beauty of what I was looking at, admiring these wonderful ladies and wondering what could have been if I had gone into modeling."

"I believe you would have been great Carol because you are beautiful, I must admit, and maybe that's why you keep getting more men to bow at your feet and do your bidding."

At first, Carol was stunned by what Jas said. She was aware that Jas had a soft spot for her but never had he been outspoken about it.

"Wow, thanks, Jas, that means a lot coming from you."

"Pleasure is all mine so any new clients yet?"

"Well, nothing yet for now considering I just got reinstated, and I had to tweak my profile a bit, just trying to rebrand and reinvent myself you know?"

"Well, sometimes I can't help but think that you are too good for this job, and your talents are probably being used in the wrong place, but it can't be helped, wish it could."

With a sigh, Carol replied, "Hmmm, I am speechless, and I don't really know what to say other than thanks."

"Well, just decided to check on you since you are back, and I hope to have updates on new set of clients very soon."

"I hope so too, thank you."

Immediately Jas left her, she bolted her door to give the impression that she was asleep. She then plugged the device into her laptop, and once she clicked it open, a sign appeared asking for name and voice verification. She clicked on the sign and announced her name, "CAROL" but nothing happened except that a voice command with the word "error" kept prompting, she was surprised, and suspected that maybe she had pronounced the name wrongly, she carefully pronounced it again only to be greeted with the same response with the addition this time that a warning was prompted stating 'one more trial and this device self-destructs'.

She could feel the stress and anxiety as she tried to figure out what the appropriate name was in order to crack the file successfully, *Wait am I supposed to use Evelyn's name to crack this damn code? Fuck I can't imagine what another passcode to use*, she thought to herself in desperation. As she was about to reach a decision to use Evelyn's name, she heard David's voice prompting. She took a deep breath to calm herself as she announced the name, 'Jamie Tan' and with that, she managed to crack the code with a green bar flashing the word 'Successful' in bold letters. She heaved a sigh of relief as she watched the device open up showing two sets of files. The first one was tagged 'Jamie' while the other, 'Danger' and without thinking for a second, she clicked on the file with her name and instantly a collage of pictures of her with snapshots of her credit cards, social security number and other forms of identification appeared on the screen. She just kept scrolling and swiping as she went through some of the footage, the ones taken with her kids, some of her at the shopping mall, and a footage of her with her mom. There were also footages the Syndicate agent that had crossed path with her and completely robbed her of her identity. At that point, she couldn't contain her emotions as tears started flowing down her cheeks. Memories of her past started to trigger in her mind, confirming the nightmare she had experienced before she left for the European assignment to bail Bertrand out. Immediately she pulled herself together to remind herself, *I am stronger now, and I am gonna make them pay.*

The file contained virtually everything she needed to know about her life and on completing the collage with stories of her, there was a red blink below the last footage flashing the sentence, 'file will be destroyed and disintegrated in 5 seconds.' The screen became fuzzy as the file splintered from view only to be replaced by a message which displayed for a few seconds before becoming completely wiped off from the screen. The Message read I GUESS YOU HAVE SEEN EVERYTHING, AND YOU SHOULD KNOW WHAT TO DO. Carol replied confidently to herself, 'For sure.'

FORTY
Blast From The Past

David was sitting at a restaurant waiting to meet up with a friend of his from the Bureau. He was quietly sipping his wine and spending every minute checking his watch. He was not ready to be caught off guard. He discovered through his brother that one of his old friends, Carter, was with the FBI and managed to track his friend down. As he looked up, he saw his friend approaching and noticed he was accompanied by a someone. Immediately they got to where David was seated and shook hands. Carter, started the conversation.

"Hello, David, sorry I am late, got tied up at work."

"It's alright, you're here now, and that's what that matters."

"This is my friend, Kevin, and believe me, when I tell you he is an asset to your cause."

"And what exactly does Kevin do and how will he be an asset to me?"

"Well, let me put it this way, both of you have something in common and are aligned on the same path, just be patient and hear him out."

David merely touched his jaw and nodded, "So, what can you do to help me solve this mind boggling case?"

Carter smiled before replying, "Up till now we didn't have a clue where the exact location of the Syndicate's base of operations was, and now we only know that it's somewhere between Goldsboro and Durham in North Carolina. It's not too far from where we are, possibly less than about 200 miles from here."

Carter googled the location from where they were in Virginia to Goldsboro on his phone to confirm the distance.

"Well, that sounds like progress, I mean North Carolina is like the closest state to Virginia," said David, "at least we know the state those son of a bitches are located now, and I can get my woman back."

"What if I could get us a step closer and get you all the necessary info to take down these guys?" asked Kevin.

"And how do you intend on pulling that off because I know these people well enough to understand the fact that they do cover their tracks excellently. You know what, scratch that. What exactly is your interest in this because if I am going to be collecting information from you, then I need to know your motives," replied David.

Carter intervened, and as he was about to comment, Kevin tapped him on the shoulder to assure them "Not to worry, he is right to ask questions and who wouldn't considering nobody can be trusted these days. Anyway, David, you may think you don't know me, but you do, cross path quite a long time ago when we were kids."

At that point, David adjusted in his seat and on noticing that he had David's attention, Kevin continued.

"Remember that foster home in Colorado where there was this stubborn kid that constantly got into trouble and almost fell to his death during one of his tantrums," he paused as he waited for a reaction from David.

David looked up and thought for a moment, even though he had always wanted to erase most of his childhood memories, he couldn't forget the day he had saved a young boy of his age from jumping to his death all in the name of trying to rebel against the way they were treated at the foster home.

Kevin was about six or seven years old then and from the first day he entered the orphanage, he was trouble. He picked a fight with the first boy he sat with and had to be punished. He seemed to have a knack for breaking the rules. He had a habit of jumping down from his room to the ground on the exterior of the building, although he was caught and punished several times he kept retaliating over and over again. One day he was running about and attempted to escape again. Instinctively, David ran after him and just as he was about to jump, he pulled him back, and both of them fell to the ground. As Kevin was about to curse and shout at David for stopping him, the latter shouted back at him, forced his head to face the ground below and ordered Kevin to "Look down and see where that fall will lead you to."

Lo and behold, there were shards of glasses planted in the area where he was going to land and immediately Kevin thanked him, held him close and they established a bond from then on. However, that bond didn't last long because David was soon adopted by a loving Canadian couple and it didn't take long before Kevin ran away and was eventually picked up from the streets by the man he eventually started calling Father.

"Welcome back," said Carter.

"So are you telling me that you are my long lost friend?"

"Yes, brother that's me, and if it weren't for you, I would not be standing here today. So when Carter told me about you and showed me your picture, I recognized you immediately, and I knew it was time to use that bond to good effect," said Kevin.

David was speechless. He was sure he couldn't take down the Syndicate all by himself, but he was determined to get Jamie out or dirtying, butut now with what seem to be reliable help right before him, he still had reservations whether Kevin was able to provide him the kind of help he would need. *Guess it's always positive to do good deeds and touch people's lives anywhere you are,* David thought to himself before finally finding the right words to reply.

"Fine, I'll bite."

"Well, for starters, I have one of their agents working for me, and I should have their authentic location within the next couple of days," said Kevin.

"I've got a slight problem with that since he can sell out the group of people he has been working with for a while, what is to say that he won't stab you in the back as well considering you're trying to bring down his source of livelihood?"

"Good observation, David," said Carter. "He has a point, you know, I mean he can change his mind at the last minute and all your plans will be a total mess," Carter reiterated to Kevin.

"Your concerns are well founded, but I have gotten absolute assurance. Carter, remember the device that was used to murder that Serbian politician by Amir Sayed about 3 years ago and how you guys couldn't totally figure out how he was killed?"

"Yes, I remember Kev, even though the case remained an unsolved mystery due to a lack of cooperation from the Serbian government."

"Well, I investigated this with my dad and discovered the name of that device. It bears a code-name, XCAPT... It's a device that goes straight to the hypothalamus of the brain once it penetrates the human body and the second it's activated, it brings about a vibration which the brain is unable to withstand, causing it to literally blow the person's brains out."

"Damn! No wonder we were not given access to the body. In fact, the photos of that body, as well as all the evidence leading to that particular case, were wiped out by the Serbian government, and now I know why," said Carter.

"Anyway, what has that got to do with the question David asked you?" Carter asked.

"Well, since I decided to step things up a notch in my vendetta against the Syndicate, I met with the scientist from Serbia, who offered me XCAPT, but he disappeared soon after. He decided to repay me for a huge favor I had done and offered me the last two of that device he had left. Though I still had to pay a heavy price for it, but now it looks like it's come in handy for us. I injected it in the agent working for me, and I gave him a little demonstration to show him that the device is not a joke. Satisfied now?"

"Well, I knew you were badass, but I never knew you could be this resourceful," said David feeling a little more cheerful and convinced Kevin was going to be of great help in finding his beloved Jamie.

"You know what they say, desperate situation calls for desperate measures, and I think we are in quite a desperate situation if you ask me. Wouldn't you agree?"

Instinctively, both Carter and David nodded their heads. Carter had initially told Kevin the FBI wasn't going to be of much help unless the latter could come up with concrete evidence when he first came to him seeking his help about taking down the Syndicate. Since then Kevin had been working on the best possible solution to take down the scumbags who had killed his Evelyn and was confident he was now getting closer to destroying the Syndicate.

"I'll leave you gentlemen to discuss more. My lunch break is over, and I gotta run." Carter said standing up and shaking both of their hands before making his exit.

Back at the Syndicate Headquarters

Douglas was working on his system surfing the Internet as available clients seem to have reduced since the incident in Germany but he was not bothered as such had happened before, and they managed to conquer and made it through. He kept surfing the Internet trying to seek for anything on Amir Sayed as well as nice places to take a vacation. As he was doing this, he stumbled upon a picture, and he scrolled down and further clicked on the details. What he saw baffled him, lying down there with is head blown off was an American Arab with the tattoo of a rattle snake on his arm and then another picture by the side but of a different man looking like an Eastern European just with the caption, 'A serial head bomber on the loose, are we safe?'

He wasn't bothered by the European man but was especially concerned about the Arab with the tattoo because everyone in the group knew the only person rumored to have such a tattoo on his arm was... *Is Amir Sayed dead? If he is who could have killed him? Then who was the one who captured me and blackmail me to work for him? Who the fuck is this person? I need to know more.* He just shut down the laptop and left the room feeling confused.

FORTY-ONE
Hanging By A Thread

As he was deep in thoughts that night, Douglas kept tossing and turning on his bed feeling uneasy. He had no idea which organization had blackmailed him to betray Rachel and the Syndicate, which had given him a purpose in life and the opportunity to develop his talent, *Yes, they may have given me a direction in life, but I've been regarded no more than a tool. Yes, I was once regarded as a lieutenant, but I was never accorded that respect which was why I'd always wanted to keep a distant from everyone. And despite all my advances towards Rachel, she paid no attention to me and always showed a preference towards Bertrand, well, guess they deserve whatever they have got coming then.* He psyched himself to wipe out the guilt he was feeling.

These were the thoughts running through Douglas' mind, but he was still in a rut as to who had posed as Amir Sayed, *Or could there be a possibility Amir Sayed fake his own death?* He wondered. *No, that can't be possible.* His head was completely blown off, and it was the tattoo that gave a clue that that was Amir Sayed because not too many people knew about his uniquely designed tattoo. Douglas was one of the few to know about it because he helped out one of Sayed's Lieutenant with a system glitch which would have gotten him killed had Douglas not been there. Douglas had then taken that as an opportunity which he later exploited to get to know a little more about Amir Sayed. His train of thoughts led him to recall that he still had a way to contact that same lieutenant, he jumped off from his bed, took out an SAT phone and dialed the number which was answered on the second ring.

"Hello?"

"Yes, who is this?" answered the crude voice on the other end of the line.

"This is Douglas from the syndicate, is this Habeeb?"

"Even if I am Habeeb, I don't know any fucking Doglass from anywhere, get off the phone for me idiot," he had always pronounced Douglas as Doglass in his Arab accent.

As Habeeb was about to hang up, Douglas remembered the phrase that Habeeb taught him during their encounter and immediately he recited it.

"Eayan alnnamr tataharrak fi alzzll," which translated in English as 'The eye of the tiger roaming in the shadows.'

Immediately the man replied and said, "Is that you my friend Dog, sorry I just have to be extra conscious this time. There's a bomb going around and people are being killed off one by one so I just have to be on alert."

Douglas' jaw dropped and, "Any idea who is responsible for the deaths?"

"Not sure but all I know is that the method Amir Sayed used to kill a certain politician in Serbia was also tried to use on him right there in Serbia, but somehow he found a way to escape though he made it look like the attempt was successful and once that happened, he disappeared, and I have not heard from him since. So right now, I don't have much covering around me, and I believe you can now understand the hostility I initially displayed."

"Yes, I do. Wow, this is serious."

"I guess that was why you called me right? You stumbled on the news about his death because those involved have tried to keep it under wraps."

"Yes, exactly and I needed to know because he seems to be out for some sort of revenge against us."

"Oh, well, you should be careful on that end like I said, he has disappeared since then but one thing is for sure, he always collects his debts."

This sent shivers down his spine. *It really is Amir Sayed*, he thought.

"You have been helpful Habeeb, and I really appreciate that."

"Well, I am glad I could help you out, my friend. I hope we don't speak again anytime soon."

With that, the line went dead. The conversation with Habeeb didn't help much as Douglas was now even more confused with regard to the status of Amir Sayed. This time, it seemed as though Amir had actually faked his own death and he was not messing around. Douglas was certain the device injected into his body was definitely not a joke. Time was running out, and Douglas felt all the more anxious to give Amir Sayed what he had asked for to prevent himself from getting blown up any time soon.

However, he was going to conduct more findings about any other surprise enemies lying in wait for the Syndicate, yes he was betraying them, but he was not going to leave them in a lurch. So he began his investigation, trying to go through some files to see if he could narrow down those they might have crossed. When he saw the list, it was enormous, and it was obvious it wasn't going to be a walk in the park. He decided to fight exhaustion to discover more through his research that night.

By dawn, Douglas was still on his system working on the list and with some criteria set, he began to reduce the list as he kept working till the list was down to 6 and apart from Amir Sayed, one other name struck him, a name he had not seen or heard in quite a while, and that was Evelyn. Though she was never regarded as an enemy but since Syndicate had a part in killing her fiancé, and with her sudden disappearance from the face of the earth, everyone just assumed that she had died in the fire that razed their building in Houston, Texas.

She had obviously hidden herself well, and while she had changed her appearance, he could not mistake her for someone else, there was just something unique about her jaw that he couldn't forget. *Wait a minute, could it be that Evelyn knew something about Carol's kidnap? But to what means? Well, don't know yet but at least a clue. Now let me get this man the info he needs before he blows my brains out.* Douglas thought to himself.

FORTY-TWO
Cold-Hearted Bastard

"Hey man, what're you doing?" beamed Jas in his normal voice and for a moment Douglas was scared because he was extracting information for the supposed Amir Sayed but he had been smart enough to cover it up with the list of Syndicate enemies that he was working on.

So immediately Jas spoke, he smiled and answered him, "Remember how everything has been a little topsy-turvy for us here, I have been trying to figure out the external forces that might be against us and know if we need to make a move ourselves."

"Well I thought it was Amir Sayed that was responsible for the kidnap of Carol, and he should be the one that we should be looking out for."

"Newsflash my friend, I think it might be a little bit more complicated than that. I still don't have all the facts yet, but I am working on it. Hopefully, I will have something concrete soon."

Jas then left and went to Carol's station hoping to meet her there, but he didn't so he went to check her in the room and met her there.

"Hey Carol, what are you doing?"

"Hey, Jas a little good morning Carol will not kill you, you know."

"My bad, forgive my rudeness, good morning Carol, hope you slept well. Now, what are you working on?"

"I just acquired a new client, and I am talking with him right now, and your intrusion is affecting my flow and my mojo."

"Well, let me see then."

Jas moved closer to check what Carol was doing and seeing it was as she said.

"Are you sure it was Amir Sayed that captured you?"

Having been prepared already by Evelyn for a situation like this, she said "Well I don't know and moreso I never said he was the one, I mean it's not like my kidnappers shook my hand and introduced themselves to me 'Hey, Carol, we have kidnapped you and our names are so and so. Forgive me if I don't know their names and why the suspicion all of a sudden. I just got an agènt–No a top dog of this organization out of a tight spot and the next thing I get rewarded with is suspicions. You think I planned my kidnap, fine then. Guess I now have the resources to do that and the people to do that and if I were to do it, it would have involved you and Douglas since you are both powerful, and he is good with IT. So if you have nothing else to accuse me of, can you please leave me to be in peace and get back to my work?"

Rachel was passing by at the time and heard Carol talking. She decided to open the door and check what was happening.

"Carol, what's going on? Or should I say, Jas what's happening?"

"Well, Jas came in and thought I had something to do with my kidnap, and I told him that if that were true, then he and Douglas would know something about it since they are next in line to you regarding authority."

"Okay Carol, I am sorry about that, but you can't blame him, we have not been able to make much headway in that direction, and he's only trying to avoid the repeat of a terrible event that occurred some years ago. And Jas, please apologize to her and let her be."

With that, they both left her room but rather than be so happy and jubilate, Carol was even more wary and careful. She faced her newly found client that seems to have fallen in love with her. He was the spoilt brat of a very rich business man from Ukraine, and he had money to burn. He so much fitted the profile of the kind of people Carol was looking to swindle. She had set up herself as a young lady of about 20 years old based in Kiev. From her conversation with the guy, she found out that he was 30, loved drinking, spending money, was a pervert, and most of all was quite dumb. All he cared about was money, booze, and women.

"Perfect!" she exclaimed.

Later in the evening, Douglas received a call, it was the man who needed the information again,

"Hello, do you have what I need or do I need to blow your brains out?"

"I have a feeling that you will not do that because you really need this information and I am your only chance."

Realizing that Douglas might be trying to play him to spill a secret of his, he simply smiled and replied, "Well I am sure you still want to get out of where you are considering the woman you want and care about does not want you, she doesn't even look at you talk less of giving you her attention."

For a moment, Douglas was silent and at the other end, Kevin knew he had struck a nerve, and he knew that he just needed to wait for his response which was just going to be positive.

"Fine, you win. You will get your info tomorrow, and you better have my ticket and the deactivator for whatever it is you put in my head."

"Sure thing, no problem. As long as you keep your end of the bargain, then I will keep mine."

The call was ended and just as he was about to get out of the restroom where he went to receive the call, he was accosted by Jas.

"What you doing with the phone man?"

"None of your business and last I checked, you don't monitor me and neither do I answer to you," replied Douglas angrily.

"Yes, I know that but all the same, you have got something fishy going on and I think you are trying to shift the blame on somebody else, that person being Carol."

"You really think you have everything figured out eh, well, guess again because you're totally wrong, and you know nothing about me or what I can or cannot do. So if you know what is good for you, just let me be and get out of my way."

Just as he made his move to leave, Jas dragged him back. Now Jas was stronger and bigger than Douglas, but Doug was smarter.

"You are not walking away from me until you answer my question, or I will drag you straight to Rachel."

It was as if Douglas' brain went into overdrive on hearing that and immediately he went on his knees and made to plead with Jas and as soon as he noticed that the hold on him had reduced, he took a knife from his boot and stabbed Jas on the thighs before moving to his stomach. He could not even react until it was too late and while he struggled with Doug to try and hit him, he couldn't do much. The wound had taken a lot of blood from him.

Douglas had knew exactly where to stab and all Jas could mutter was, "You cold-hearted bastard."

"Say whatever you want, whose heart is cold right now?"

Immediately he called back the number that just called him and explained what just happened.

"I'm in danger man, and I have the needed info, but if you don't get me out now, the information will be lost, and I will be killed. Traitors aren't exactly given a high welcome here."

No problem, can you make it to Goldsboro tonight? Once you get there, call me, I will be waiting for you."

Instantly, he moved Jas' body to a secure place in the restroom and quickly went to pick his load that he had packed before sneaking out of the building. He had to go on foot so as not to alert the guards and so he began to run which was not difficult for him because he went for jogs regularly and as such was familiar with the terrain.

He eventually got to the main road and stole a car off of someone and began the drive to Goldsboro. After about 45 minutes of driving, he got to the meeting point, in fact, they were already waiting for him. He got down off the car and approached.

"Well, here's what you asked for as well as all the codes needed to hack their accounts to transfer their money. Now where is what I asked for?"

"It will have to be tested for authentication and to be sure it's not some sort of virus."

"Okay fair enough, just be quick about it because I need to be out of the country tonight. Hope you got my ticket."

"I did you one better, I have got you a standby ticket to Panama, which means you can leave tonight if you want."

All the while, Douglas could not see the face of the man that was talking to him, but he now was convinced more than ever that it was Amir Sayed because he always kept his word despite his black heart.

"Confirmed Sir," said one of the people checking out the file.

"Alright, thanks. Give him his ticket and envelope and let him go."

Expecting him to leave, he spoke and said, "What more do you want, our deal is over isn't it?"

"Well, there's still that thing in my head, and I think part of the deal was deactivating it."

"Oh yes, and then Kevin pressed a button on the device with him and deactivated the XCAPT capsule on Douglas' head.

"Well, now you can go, the device will dissolve and will be passed out as waste product from your body so, that way you're safe."

"Fine, but one more thing."

"What more could you possibly want cockroach?"

"Well, I got news for you, and since we won't see again, I might just spill it. You remember the girl we sent out a contract for the death of her boyfriend, well, she seems to be alive and might be interested in ruining your revenge plan because she seems to be on her own vendetta against the Syndicate as well. That's the more reason I took your deal because if she sees me, she will not show me the mercy you just showed me."

Kevin was stunned, but he quickly recovered and said, "That's bogus. I mean she was your problem in the first place, and you couldn't take care of her but why should I expect anything better from a cockroach?"

He spit and said, "Rubbi..." but before he could finish the statement, Douglas threw a mass storage device at him.

"Check that out."

He then turned his back and entered the vehicle he brought, "Nice doing business with you."

FORTY-THREE
Fresh Discovery

"Hey Tina, when do I get to see those beautiful tits and ass of yours?"

"Well, when do you want to see everything?"

"Can you show me now? I am so horny right now and seeing your body will satisfy me."

At this point, Carol paused and smiled because she had the 'fool' exactly where she wanted him, and she was already prepared for this. But then it was a service she was about to render, and there had to be payment for it. So she decided to tease him a little bit further...

"Baby, I am also horny for you and I can't wait to show you what I am packing underneath this dress."

"Oh, baby, now you are getting me hard. Please just let me see you."

Meanwhile, Carol had prepared pictures that she would send to him, and she sent the first one to him.

"Damn it, baby, these tits are awesome, I wish I could touch them right now. Oh, give me more baby."

"Well, if you need more, you will have to pay for its love, nothing comes cheap and only the first one is free."

"Okay, I knew you might bring that up, and I am prepared for it, so how much am I looking at so that I can send it to you."

Carol again took a deep breath and while she was sure that he would meet her demands, she didn't want to appear forward or too demanding and throw him off. So she decided to throw it back at him:

"Well, how much are you willing to pay? I mean if it's precious to you, then you might as well put up something with value."

"How about if I give you 50,000€ for a start, and if you make me happy, then I will add more. Just send me the necessary account details."

"Alright, I will then."

She gave him the account number and just as she finished typing, she heard a commotion not far from her room, but she ignored it at first but then it kept growing, so she decided to check it out. In fact, as she was coming out, someone almost ran into her and knocked her down, but she was able to avoid it. Now sensing that there was real trouble because never had there been this much noise or confusion ever since she had started working for the Syndicate, she went straight down the lobby to the main room and right there was Rachel pacing about staring at something in front of her. So she decided to move further and take a closer look, to her surprise and horror, she saw Jas lying on the floor with a knife stuck in him.

"What? Who could have done this?" exclaimed Carol.

Her voice seemed to bring Rachel to the awareness of another person in the room and immediately she turned around, "Oh Carolena, at the moment I don't know, but we are reviewing the tapes to get an idea but you know some parts of the building do not have cameras like the restroom where his body was found. So right now, I have no idea who is responsible."

Then Carol moved closer and looked at the knife because it looked familiar and immediately her brain went into overdrive trying to figure out where she had seen the knife before and whom she had seen it with. Then she remembered the day she was passing by Doug's room when he was almost through with dressing up and she noticed him placing a knife in his boot. When she had started to questions him, he'd simply smiled and said, 'For luck.'

She just shrugged her shoulders and left because for one, Douglas rarely smiled and definitely not at or with Carol, so while she was surprised, she didn't give it much thought considering she had been told that Doug was just an eccentric guy, and it's better to let him be.

"It's Doug, it had to be him," Carol exclaimed.

Immediately, Rachel rose to his defense, "Carol, you had better be careful with such accusations. Why would you say Douglas killed Jas when he would have already left for his morning jog? How am I sure that you're not the one responsible for this?"

Carol unmoved simply smiled and replied to Rachel, "Really, are you sure Douglas has gone for a jog or started a journey with no plans to return? That knife belongs to him because I have seen it with him before and he told me it's for luck. Guess it brought him luck and death to Jas."

Rachel still not believing sent two men to check out the jogging path which

Douglas normally took while the tape was being reviewed.

"Why not just check out the tapes of the camera in Douglas' workstation." prompted Carol.

"Fine, pull up the tape from his workstation like she said."

Immediately the tape was pulled up, and the conversation Jas had with Douglas was there as well as the part where he challenged Douglas about what he was doing and the way he deflected it onto someone else. While this was on, a thought occurred to Rachel that they should try and check a record of the activities of Douglas on the system and to her surprise, it had been erased except for the last two transactions in which he transferred some of the funds to Amir Sayed.

"Ma'am, check this out."

Rachel then took a closer look and she couldn't believe what she was seeing. About a million Euros had just been transferred, and he was smart enough to mask them until it was too late. The account to which it was sent was untraceable.

Douglas had wiped all the past transactions he had made, and he was on the verge of wiping this last one as well, but that was when he went to receive the call in which Jas accosted him before he eventually killed Jas. That might have given him insufficient time to completely wipe out all evidence because he was rushing to get out and avoid being caught.

"I can't believe this but why would Douglas betray us, betray me after everything my family and I have done for him? We took him in when he was nothing, gave his life a purpose and sense of direction and all he could do is betray me, he even killed Jas." Rachel was seriously angry and pounded her fists on the table.

Eventually, the men came back and gave her the report, "We couldn't find anything ma'am, in fact, there were no tracks. It's as if he never went on a run this morning."

"Thank you. You're dismissed."

"Yes, ma'am."

"Get his body to the morgue and tell them to clean him up. He is going to have a proper burial because he was a loyal servant and it's the least we can do for him."

"Yes, ma'am."

Rachel immediately went to her office because she was moved to tears though feeling very angry at the same time. She vowed to hunt down Douglas and make him pay, but something deep within her told her that it might not be entirely possible, a thought she tried to shrug off.

FORTY-FOUR
The New Bodyguard

A memorial service was finally held in Jas' honor, and he was laid to rest. So the syndicate headquarters just lost its best tech expert and the most trusted personal bodyguard to the head of operations. Talk about a double sucker punch and to have it come from one of your own. Rachel was really bothered about it, and it just seemed as if everything was going against her. She was not one that believed in natural forces or supernatural ones for that matter but she herself couldn't help but admit it that it looked like those forces were definitely at work against her.

"I simply don't understand what's going on, I mean first Bertrand was captured, now Jas is dead, and Douglas has disappeared into thin air. This is just too much for me alone to bear. Now I need to get another trusted lieutenant, where do I start from? I don't want to ask other branches for help, I will only come across as weak to them."

Just then Carol walked in, "I didn't mean to disturb you, ma'am, maybe I will come some other time when you're in a better mood."

"No, stay. I think I need the company. It might do me some good rather than just keep to myself and probably suffer from depression."

"Alright, as you wish then. I am really sorry about Jas' death. He was a sweet guy and even though he looked so tough on the outside, inside he was soft and caring. Wish I got to know him more. "

"Well same here, I got so used to his presence that I was taking him for granted at a point, but still, he was loyal and would have given his life for me. Oh, poor Jas."

Rachel was practically crying, and Carol had to move closer to her to hug. She was reluctant to offer at first thinking that Rachel might refuse the gesture, but she took it openly and just rested on Carol's shoulder before Carol reached to hand her a tissue to wipe the running mascara from her eyes.

"Thank you Carol, and I am sorry for the way I have treated you initially."

"Oh, it's alright, I got your back, and I will not stop giving my best to this organization."

"Well, Carol I must admit that you have been one constant face throughout this whole crisis, and I hope you will continue to have my back."

"Definitely, I promise."

And for a moment, Carol wished she could believe what she just said, but she knew within herself that it was not going to happen. The Syndicate had taken so much from her, and they were going to pay for it no matter what it took.

So a few weeks later, everything seemed to have died down, and everyone was back to their duty posts, but still, it could be felt that certain elements were missing from the wheel of operation. But what could anyone do other than to move on and continue with their work? Eventually, Rachel had to reach out and get a new bodyguard from one of the other branches, but she still preferred to confide in Carol because she was the closest thing she had at the moment.

Carol continued with her careful selection of clients, and after she was done with the guy from Ukraine whose money was used to finance some things within the Syndicate, she relaxed a little bit more expecting another right client but this time hoping for a 'bigger fish' than the last one. She checked through the likes and messages that she had, but she was just scrolling through them all to find that none interested her. Finally, she stopped on one, she didn't know why but he really struck her, and she intended to know him more. So she clicked on his profile and checked him out. He was tall about 6'2", black curly hair and a well-chiseled face. She was not one to fall for men easily not after her experiences with the Syndicate, but this one certainly intrigued her. Noticing that he was online, she decided to send him a message *"Hello handsome."*

At first, she didn't get a response and so that she didn't come across as pushy, she decided not to send another message to him. Then not quite long afterwards, she got a message which she clicked on.

"Hi, Kate or am I wrong about your name?"

Carol replied immediately *"Nope that's my name as obvious from the username. I am guessing yours is Devon right?"*

"Yes, definitely. So I must say you really are beautiful, and I would really like to get to know you better."

"Well, it will be my pleasure."

They kept chatting and gradually began to know each other more. Carol was not yet sure of what she would be getting from him, but she was only being drawn along by curiosity. For weeks they both continued getting to know one another and by that time, Carol had made some deeper findings of her own about Devon. She discovered some revealing things which made her continue to be in contact with him. For starters, his real name was Sylvain, an Albanian raised in the United States. He was into drugs but loved women, and he did everything to get different varieties of them, which was part of the reason why he registered on online dating platforms. She also discovered that he had been involved in a few murders. The last part scared Carol a little before she thought to herself, *What's life without a little danger?* So finally, they decided to meet at a restaurant in Durham because he happened to be based in North Carolina and this was where Carol knew she had to make her final move. She started thinking, *How do I get this thing done? I cannot afford to get caught because if I do, I might as well forget about getting revenge on the Syndicate and also forfeit my life. I can't do this alone. I am going to need a little help. Let me go talk to Rachel and inform her about it.*

So she went to Rachel's office and knocked, "Come in."

She entered and sat down.

"So any problem Carol?"

"No, not at all, just came to discuss an important matter with you because I need your help to accomplish it successfully."

"Alright, I am all ears."

She explained it all to Rachel about how he wanted to meet. She also told her that she would like to make it a one-time move and then not see him again.

"Okay Carol, I must admit that it's a tricky one considering what you have told me about him, but I think there's only one person who can help you pull that off, and her name is Talia. She's in the logistics section, just tell her I sent you and explain everything to her."

"Thanks a lot. I hope to provide you with good news soon."

She left Rachel's office and went to look for Talia. Once she located, she explained everything to her, and they both came up with a plan. Tuesday the following week was the day of the date. Carol agreed to meet him at around 2:00pm and because of the sun, she had to wear sunglasses. When she got there, he was already waiting for her. He just stood up and greeted her, opening his arms for a hug which she gladly obliged except for the fact that he took it a step further by grabbing her butt.

"Welcome," he said, "that's a nice ass you got there."

Well, be careful what you wish for, Carol told herself.

Flanking him were two bodyguards as expected by Carol but it was obvious pulling this off was not going to be a walk in the park.

"So what would you like to eat?" asked Devon.

"On second thought, why not have what I am having. Waiter, make it two of what I am having and add a bottle of white wine to it."

Controlling and manipulative, how convenient, Carol thought again.

And as if reading her mind, he said, "Hope you don't mind. I just like taking charge of things with my women, and I believe you would like to be mine right?"

"Yes, I would love to," Carol said with a smile.

Their orders were brought, and they began eating and talking.

"You know you look more beautiful in person than in the picture, and I wish I had met you sooner. But I guess it's not too late, though."

"No, it's not. In fact, your timing could not have been more perfect."

Looking more curious and interested, Devon moved closer and asked, "How so?"

"Well, I am at a period of my life where everything is in shambles, and I just need a man that will take charge and give me some meaning," replied Carol.

"Guess I am your knight in shining armor then. I've always been told I had impeccable timing like when I was born, that was when my parents were eventually able to move to the US after years of trying."

"Wow, amazing."

After eating, he paid with his credit card and Carol smiled within herself, this was exactly what she was waiting for, and it really seemed special because he didn't just keep it in his wallet, it was like he really kept it close to himself, his jacket's breast pocket to be precise. After that, they both stood up and left.

"So when will I get to see you again and whatever it is under that dress?"

Carol felt disgusted but not surprised, Devon always spoke his mind and gave little or no thoughts to manners.

She simply smiled and said, "Whenever you decide, I will oblige and let you do whatever you please with me."

"Well, how about today?"

"Oh come on, not today...."

"Ah, just kidding. At least I now have your number so I can call you."

"Yes, you can."

"So why don't I drop you off on my way."

"Don't worry, brought my own ride."

"Hmm, a beautiful, confident and independent woman, I like that."

"Thanks."

Carol drove off and just as she did, a young lady passed by and collapsed as a result of the heels she was wearing and then he helped her up and adjusted her dress which had moved slightly exposing her thighs in the fall. She smiled as she thanked him. He smiled at her back and drove off straight to his house. He changed, and began patting his body down having the sneaking suspicion that something was missing, it hit him like thunder! His platinum credit card that was linked to his main account where he was expecting a payment that day of around 2 million dollars.

"No, that card can't be lost like that, I kept it well. Spiff, Tyler, my card is missing, find it or don't come back."

Immediately they ran out and began to look for the card, they checked the car, inside, underneath, in fact, checked the tires in case it got stuck on it but can you blame them? It was either the card or their lives.

After hours of searching and even driving around town trying to locate the card and looking like madmen in doing so, they came back to their boss guns drawn and ready to kill themselves.

"Sorry, boss we looked all over town but couldn't find it, we are deeply sorry but since you said we should not come back alive give us the dignity of shooting ourselves."

Just as he was about to answer and tell them to get on with it, the second guard spoke, "Boss, maybe you can try to review the events of the day."

At this point, he calmed himself and went over the events, mumbling to himself as he went.

"Well I paid and after paying, I put the card back in my pocket, and I entered the car.... No before then I helped a young lady, but could it be? No, thieves are not that well-dressed. But..."

"Don't kill yourselves, I will get the account blocked and remove my money though it might take some time, but either way, fuck man! Damn that bitch in hell!

At the Syndicate, Talia and Carol were applauding one another and had already been working on the card and transferring all the available funds which amounted to a whopping $2.5 million. What a break it was for Carol. Rachel was delighted when she heard the news.

"Damn girl, you rock. Talia, now you get a promotion and Carol, you have a workstation not far from me."

This was what Carol had wanted all along, and now, she can put it into full swing.

FORTY-FIVE
Deja Vu

Back in Prague, Bertrand was busy with operations but since getting back from Germany, things had not exactly been the same or gone as planned. Realizing that this might put a stop to his extravagant lifestyle, he decided to branch out into drugs and arms. He wasn't a user of drugs but he didn't care as long as he could make bank. So he started dealing and with time was making crazy money even more than when he was simply swindling people. With this, life was back to normal for Bertrand and all of a sudden, he seemed to have gotten over his arrest by the German authorities; life couldn't be better. Just then his phone rang.

"Hello, who am I speaking with?"

"I hope this is the Eagle. My name is of no significance but the man who sent me."

"So who did?" asked Bertrand.

"The Sparrow. He said to ask if you have any consignment on ground and how soon he can get it."

"Right now, I don't have one, but it should be ready in 2-3 days if that's not too long."

"That's perfect, exactly the time he needs it. He's looking to get about 50 kilos if that will be possible."

"Well, that will be possible and even if he needs more, I can provide that. So is it still the same price of $40,000 per kilo."

"Yes it is, and if well delivered with no problem whatsoever, then there is going to be a tip for you."

Bertrand's eyes widened at the thought of a tip. Now the Sparrow was paranoid in his dealings which was typical of a Mexican-born drug lord residing in the Czech Republic, but he was generous as long as you maintained your own end of the deal. So naturally on top of the two million dollars that was on the brink for him, there was a tip of not less than $100k-$200k.

"Well, I will do my best to get it across. Account is the same, and you know the process."

"Yes, I remember. Half will be transferred to you now and the other half on completion of the delivery."

With that, the call was ended and not long after, there was a message on Bertrand's phone which he read.

"$1,000,000 has been transferred to your account."

Bertrand got to work and calling his contacts to provide what he needed. Now Bertrand usually got his cocaine from Colombia because it was neat and clean without much hassle. Also, he bought a kilo for only $1,500 and sold it for between $40,000-$60,000 depending on who his buyer was. So overall it was a great business which really made him rich. Moreso, he was also generous which kept his contacts close and also meant being given a free pass with the authorities. He had met the Sparrow through one of the people he dealt with. It was the man that recommended him to the Sparrow due to the quality of his products and since then he had been dealing with him and not looked back ever since.

Two days later, he contacted the Sparrow and delivered the goods at the agreed location and after proper inspection, he was paid his balance as well as a tip of around $300,000 because he himself had thrown in an extra 5kg for free. So imagine his surprise and joy when he saw the extra money beyond what he was expecting. Immediately, he went out with a couple of friends and celebrated. *Why have money if you can't spend it,* he thought.

***

Kevin was left stunned with the information in front of him. He was staring at his long-lost fiancée that he assumed was dead, and she probably assumed the same about him.

"Evelyn's alive? How did she survive the fire?"

Immediately a voice inside him asked, *How did you survive your own assassination?*

He continued further, "How do I locate her, I mean where do I even start from?"

He decided to talk to his dad because he always seemed adept at situations like this. So he picked up the phone and dialed the familiar number.

"Hello, Dad, how are you?"

"I am fine my son. Been a while since I heard from you. Hope you are making progress on the project?"

"Actually, I am, and that's why I called you."

"Is anything the matter cos you sound worried?"

"Yes, there is as a matter of fact."

"Okay, I am listening."

"Well, do you remember my fiancée then, Evelyn?"

"Yes, I do."

"Well, I just discovered she's alive, and she seems to be fighting against her former employers."

"Wait a minute, do you mean it? So where is she?"

"Therein lies the problem, I don't know precisely where, but I just have places where she has been sighted."

"How did you get the information?"

"Through one of the agents of the group she was working for. In case you are wondering, I got him to turn and betray his own people and then he dumped the information on my lap."

"Well, the places she has been should serve as a compass for you to locate where she might be or maybe she just doesn't want to be found until she's ready."

"But I need to find her. I am happy and a little sad at the same time because it feels good to know she's still alive but not happy I can't locate her."

"Don't worry about that, just look deeper and you will locate her. Trust your instincts and remember your training."

"Thanks, Dad knew you will help me with the right solution."

"Anytime son."

***

Two months later

The Sparrow was carrying out a transaction in Germany when he was arrested by the German authorities and after proper interrogation, he revealed where he got his supplies from.

"Look, I have never seen his face before and neither has he seen mine because most of our transactions are carried out on phone and wire transfer, so all that we do is arrange a location for the drop and that's all."

"Fine, you contact him, and you tell him that you need around 100 kilos by the end of the week and as usual, half will be transferred to him immediately."

So the arrangements were made, and Bertrand was told the shipment was to be brought to a location in Stuttgart and that it will be picked up there. The location for delivery had never been that far before but considering there was a private plane at his disposal, he could afford to do it and not ready to take any chances by sending someone considering the weight of the package, he decided to go himself. But that was after due consideration, remembering the case that happened in Germany a couple of months ago but this time, he was going to be more careful because he was going to be in and out before anyone knew it. He got to the drop-off point, and he was helped by two of the men whom he assumed to be the Sparrow's men. By the time they entered the warehouse and the package was inspected, they were set upon by law enforcement agents.

Bertrand cursed under his breath.

"Fuck...Not again," he muttered.

He turned around to find that the men who had inspected the package had also turned out to be law enforcement agents.

"Oh, come on, really. Fine, I give up."

Inspector Otto then walked out from the midst of the other agents.

"Well as if I knew it was you, guess there's no escape from us this time around."

With that, he was arrested and whisked away.

FORTY-SIX
Riding on The Edge

Another Two months later...

"Hello, please am I speaking with the Scorpion?"

"Yes, you are, who is asking?"

"The person asking is of little or no consequence, but the information I have for you is what matters."

"Alright, I'll bite," said Rachel, already sounding a bit anxious.

"I believe you know Bertrand right?"

"Yes, I do."

"Well, he has been arrested by the German authorities and his case has been handed over to Interpol, and no one knows where he is held at right now."

"What? How did that happen? I mean after his previous experience, I am sure he will have been more cautious?"

"Well, I heard he was arrested for Drug smuggling along with a couple of notorious drug lords, and they have been transported to a prison no one knows. So it's possible that you might not hear from him again."

Rachel could not believe what she had heard and went silent for a while. Her mind was thinking a lot of things at the same time, but she was brought back to the present by the voice at the other end of the line.

"Hello, are you still there?"

"Oh yes, I am. Just trying to digest this news that you gave me. It is really a lot to digest."

"I do understand, but I believe it's better to start watching your back at this point or better still, get someone that you trust to do that from you."

"Thanks for the advice."

The line went dead leaving Rachel thrown into a turmoil of thoughts. The last person she had regarded as family was gone just like that, *Jas is dead, and Douglas has left me in a lurch. I am practically hanging. Now, what do I do? Could it be that Carol has brought us ill-luck? I mean ever since she was captured and brought here, things have not been going so smooth.* Immediately, another voice inside of her answered her *When did you start getting superstitious? More so, has this same Carol not been the one making the highest amount of money for the organization ever since she came? What about the big paycheck she brought to you recently? Don't be ungrateful Rachel.*

Rachel then changed her line of thoughts. Not that she didn't have a new bodyguard, and he was one strong, tall and agile guy. On top of that, he was really intelligent as he had saved Rachel about 3 times over the last four months since arriving by merely using his intuition. Rachel was beginning to trust him, but he was no Jas neither was he Bertrand. *Doesn't look like I have much of a choice cos it seems like I am stuck with Vucinic,* she thought to herself.

Vucinic was her new bodyguard from one of Syndicate's branches that was sent to replace Jas. Vucinic was purely a mercenary having had military experience in the United States Armed Forces, Marines to be precise. He was about six feet tall with well-built muscular body and was definitely no pushover. His military experience had really sharpened his instinct and awareness.

His talent was undeniable, but Rachel still wished she had Jas by her side, but then again, *Beggars can't be choosy. Not much options right now.* With that, she shrugged and sent for Vucinic.

"Yes ma'am, I was told you sent for me."

"Yes, that I did. You remember Bertrand right? Our head agent in Prague."

"Yes, I do. Met him twice."

"Well, I just heard he has been arrested by Interpol on drug smuggling charges, and he has been shipped off to God knows where."

"Wait, can't we get him back. I mean we just need to find the right people from the right places."

"Well, the problem is right there. We seem to have more enemies than friends, he had been arrested by the German authorities previously and we got him out but it looks like they actually set a trap for him and the moment he slipped up, they grabbed him and then kept his location a secret."

"Now that's a serious step. So what do you propose we do then?"

"Well, for now, I only trust one person, and that's me. Yes, that may disappoint you, but right now I ain't got a choice."

"I am not particularly disappointed considering you can't afford to trust anyone else in our line of work except yourself."

"Good. Now, what I need you to do is to watch my back by simply trying to keep an eye on everyone and try to monitor their moves. Do you think you can do that?"

"Yes, I can. I was sent here to serve your interests and that's exactly what I intend to do."

Vucinic left Rachel's office and began his reconnaissance work. He was stealth as much as possible in his approach as everyone went about their day to day activities without suspecting a thing. Carol had finally established herself in the Syndicate as a force to be reckoned with, and though Rachel did not totally trust her, she still sought her out every once in a while for her opinion on some matters. Gradually, she began to set her plan in motion by copying contacts of some important agents of the Syndicate and their location and then began to send to Evelyn, who had been patiently waiting to start taking down the Syndicate. On getting the message from Carol, she set to action as her people began to work on the files to start deciphering them.

Now Carol was able to gain access to the files because she had single-handedly made funds available to the Syndicate for operation and payment of those that need to be paid. Like Rachel said, she had been the only one who had performed well consistently. That gave her a passport to have a free hand in operating. In fact, she started to help out the new set of guys in the tech department because she was now more tech-savvy than before. Unknowingly to them, Carol had been gradually adding a virus to the server, and it was affecting it systematically.

Vucinic was trying to watch her but didn't pay too much attention to her due to the close relationship she enjoyed with him until he peered into her room one day and saw her receiving a call but he couldn't pick out much from what she was saying and when he knocked and entered, she appeared a little shocked but quickly composed herself. That was when he started suspecting her and began to keep a closer look on her.

"Hey, what you doing? Who were you speaking to on the phone?"

"Just a client."

"I thought you don't give your numbers out to clients in order to prevent detection."

"Well, sometimes we make exceptions just to ensure that the client is trapped and falls for it."

Vucinic simply shrugged and said, "Okay."

Carol was relieved but with her level of paranoia, she suspected that he didn't believe her, which also meant she had to move fast. After copying all the contacts successfully, she riddled the system with the virus given to her by Evelyn and within a few days, the entire system of the Syndicate operation right at the headquarters collapsed, and a lot of important files were lost leaving them in serious rut. Instincts told Vucinic that Carol was responsible but without facts, he was not ready to make an accusation against the boss' favorite person. He asked the tech guys to review the breakdown only to discover that they were the ones that caused the crash. In fact, Douglas had already put in a fail-safe in a part of the system which Carol had been careful to avoid in which the tech guys had missed and in their bid to upgrade the system they unknowingly activated it, at least according to what the record showed.

When Rachel heard it, she remained expressionless and simply told them to go fix it with a wave of her hand. For starters, she had a backup of the contacts, and secondly, she was already tired and working on a way out for herself. *No point getting myself killed over this,* she thought.

FORTY-SEVEN
Domino Effect

Kiev, Ukraine.
"Hands up, everyone, you're all under arrest" beamed the commanding officer of the Interpol team inside the Syndicate building in Kiev. Some tried to escape but were pursued immediately until they were captured. The Interpol team met with little or no resistance since the agents were caught off guard. They were arrested with all their equipment seized by the authorities.

Prague, Czech Republic.
It was a different story as there was a power struggle within this branch. After the capture of their boss, they were on high alert even though they could never imagine their operations could be located so easily. They knew their boss had been arrested once and got out of it, and they were expecting the same this time around but after three months and no news of release of their boss, they began to prepare themselves.

Immediately the Interpol team stationed in Prague got to their location and entered, the Syndicate agents opened fire on them but even Interpol was prepared and they responded in kind. Eventually, they were able to subdue them and arrest the ones that were alive while ambulances were called to move the dead bodies.

Five days earlier...

"Good to see you again Kevin,"

"Same here David."

"Hello, I am also here, and I believe I brought you two together but all of a sudden, I am left out," pointed Carter.

"Come on man, you're hosting us now, don't be such a wuss," said Kevin.

"Wuss, really, wait till I lift you and throw you out of my house together with your information."

"Alright, fine you win then. It's so lovely to see you, Carter. How are your wife and kids."

"Well, thanks for asking Kevin, they're at my in-law 's at the moment till I am done with this whole Syndicate case. I need a vacation after this case is solved."

"Vacation, really? That sounds nice but at least, let's get down to business so we can each have our woman in our hands," interrupted David.

Kevin then brought out his laptop and showed his friends the files he had collected from Douglas, which contained the locations of various branches of the Syndicate in different countries as well as names of their top lieutenants.

David, finally smiling and with a ray of hope commented, "Well, this is what I'm talking about. When we say the Syndicate's going down, they are going down hard."

After pausing for a moment, he rested his jaw on his hands and said, "But how do we take all these branches down, I mean even if we have the capacity which we don't, it will take years for them to all be taken down and they will even get tipped off as soon as they notice other branches are going down quite rapidly–"

"–Which will defeat the purpose and make all our efforts a waste of time? Yeah well, I have been ahead of you on that front actually. I have already spoken to my boss ever since Kevin told me of his plan to get the files needed to take down this underworld organization and he promised to help. He linked me up with one of the top officers at Interpol, and I called him two days ago. His name is Bourne Thompson, and he has told me that once I have the file, that I should send it to him and work will commence immediately and simultaneously at that," Carter informed him.

"That sounds like good news and how about their headquarters here in North Carolina, how do we take care of that?" asked David.

Kevin finally commented, "My men and I together with some FBI agents, led of course by Carter, will round them up and then hand them over eventually to Interpol after full interrogation of those scumbags. If the scumbags make it tough for all of us to seize them, we have programmed a drone as a backup. Chances are we might use the drone and blow up the whole place."

"That sounds like a plan. So why don't we start sending the files and get it over with in order for us to prepare for the one that is right here under our noses because each moment Jamie spends in that place feels as though it's a day closer for me to lose her," said David.

Kevin placed his hand on his shoulder and assured him, "Don't you worry man, we are gonna get her back. We're at the final phase and getting closer to the end of the tunnel."

***

Three days later...

"C'mon people, let's get this show on the road. This list should be ready in the next 48 hours so that appropriate action can be taken."

That was Evelyn trying to encourage her people to finish up with deciphering the list Carol had sent to them. She had contacted her friend in Interpol who was also ready to swing into action once the list was made available. After 48 hours, the list was ready and immediately, Evelyn informed her contact and sent it to him. About the same time, that was when the list from Carter also came in to the same Bourne Thompson, but Evelyn's own was more comprehensive as Carol was able to gather everything while Douglas was only able to get half before Jas accosted him. The next day, Interpol swung into action, and that was when the Syndicate locations across the world were raided simultaneously, and they all got taken down except for the US branch which Kevin decided to handle with his friends, but little did they realized that branch was going to be the most challenging of all to take down.

Rachel was sitting in her office talking on the phone with one of her business partners.

"Look, Antonio, I need to get out of here because everything seems to be falling apart plus I don't think I am ready to lose my life over this, and neither does prison suit me."

"Well, I understand your fears, so what do you wanna do?"

Antonio paused expecting Rachel to reply, but there was complete silence from the other end of the conversation.

"You know you're welcome here anytime. I have been telling you to come, but you said Nigeria is boring, and we don't have the tech you guys have. True but ours is a market waiting to be explored and exploited," Antonio continued.

"Yeah, you are right, but I guess I need to leave now or face certain jail-time if I am not killed. So I will be coming over soon but make preparation for two people, though."

"Two people, guess you're bringing a friend."

"Well, more like a trusted bodyguard and he deserves a place by my side if I were to survive."

"Hmm fine, as long as he is with you and won't cause trouble. I will be expecting you soon then."

The call ended and Rachel rubbed her forehead. *It was time to move, this has gone on for too long, but I enjoyed it while it lasted*, she thought to herself.

FORTY-EIGHT
The Last Straw

When Rachel heard the news of other Syndicate branches going down to Interpol forces, she was heartbroken and guilty because everything her dad had worked for was going up in flames and there was little or nothing she could do about it. She looked at all those that were working for her and looked back to the good years they had together. She wished there were some things she had done and said when at the same time wished there were some things she could take back. This was indeed looking like the end of the road.

Jamie meanwhile was trying to tidy up the work with her because she had a feeling all hell was about to break loose after she received news from Evelyn that the branches had been taken and also the arrest of Bertrand. With the death of Jas and the disappearance of Douglas, the Syndicate headquarters was at its most vulnerable. Just like Evelyn told her the last time they spoke, 'The fruit is ripe for harvest, and there's no point in wasting time anymore.' Jamie was now focused on planning her own escape from the Syndicate.

***

4 hours later...

Evelyn had landed in a private airstrip in North Carolina and was gearing up with her people to go take down Rachel and her cohorts. She wanted to make Rachel suffer and feel her pain, just like she inflicted on her some five or six years ago and she was well prepared to see to that.

"Have you packed all that we need?"

"Yes, I have ma'am."

"Ensure you don't forget anything," continued Evelyn.

She was met by the guy that had helped her previously when the Syndicate building was burnt down in Texas. He was now a private security contractor with all the weapons you could need as well as the necessary connection.

"Welcome, you look amazing now even more than I can remember. Nice one Evelyn."

"You are not so bad yourself, Dwayne. Guess business has been treating you well?"

"Yes, it has, and I have been looking forward to this day when an end will come to this crazy organization. Thank God you are here to do just that."

"Let's just hope it all goes according to plan."

They then got into the cars provided by Dwayne and started their journey.

***

Back in Virginia, Kevin together with David and Carter were also preparing for their mission heading towards Syndicate headquarters to take them down without any of the groups knowing about each other's intentions. A two-pronged attack was in place for the same target.

When Evelyn's group got there, they set to work.

"Set the charges around the building but remember we cannot blow the building until Jamie is out okay? She is a priority and all these will not have been possible without her."

"Alright ma'am, duly noted. Let's get to work then, shall we?" said Evelyn's next in command.

Evelyn and Dwayne with a couple of others that were free began to go into the building stealthily knocking guards and sentries unconscious. Due to the building's massive size and compound in which the base of operations was located, it was tough to maneuver easily but the first room they went to was the video feed room to put in a loop and which kept displaying a particular set of video feed.

Rachel was already sensing that something was wrong while Carol had already made her move and had found her way out of the building since she had gotten the signal that the calvary had arrived. She immediately sent for Vucinic, but he had also disappeared.

"Where the fuck are the both of them? That bitch! I should have killed her long ago, and I had the feeling in my gut that she had something to do with all of these. No matter, I'm leaving."

With that, she passed through an underground tunnel that only she was aware of. Before others could realize what was happening, her chopper was up in the air and had flown away.

Evelyn was angry as she looked up at the chopper and cursed, "Shit, this fucking bitch managed to escape, not when I planned to make her pay for everything she did to me."

"Don't need to make her pay because I am here."

On hearing that familiar voice, Evelyn turned around and couldn't believe her eyes and ears.

"Is that really you Kevin?"

"Yes, it is darling in flesh and blood."

Evelyn charged to him and hugged him and didn't want to let go.

"You could have at least found a way to reach me. I cried for days thinking you were dead," said Evelyn.

"I am so sorry my love. I had to make it seem I was dead so that I could punish these people including those that tried to kill me but I had to keep you safe at the same time. Though I also assumed you were dead. But I am glad we are re-united. These are my friends David and Carter. We did this together."

"Nice meeting you guys."

Immediately, Kevin got on his knees, "Remember we were set to be married before we got separated, so Evelyn Lane, will you make me the happiest man on earth today and marry me?"

Evelyn could not believe it. She was happy and shocked at the same time. It had been a while since she had felt like this, with teary eyes, she answered.

"Yes."

Applause erupted around them.

"Guys I need to find my woman. Can you all please get back to business? We can't blow up the place yet because Jamie is definitely still in there," David shouted desperately at them as he tried putting the group back in perspective.

They started searching the entire building and were disappointed that the place was entirely abandoned while Jamie was nowhere in sight.

"Where the fuck is she? Could she have been taken away by Rachel?"

156

FORTY-NINE
BREAKING FREE

On the other hand, Jamie took the opportunity to break free from the perpetrators hours before Rachel escaped in her chopper. As she was about to get out of the building, she kept thinking of the children who have been kidnapped by the perpetrators and images of her own kids came to her mind as she recalled how she used to save her twins from being physically abused by their dad. She felt the hurt and pain for the children and was sure if she were to abandon them, those kids would be sentenced under the mercy of those scumbag perpetrators for life.

They would all abandon this place and vanish by the time I go get the cops, she thought to herself. Feeling compassionate and selfless, she decided to do what was right, she turned back into the building in an attempt to save the kids.

She looked for Jose and the rest of the boys who were always hanging out with him and spotted them going through some wallets and purses they had picked that day. She signaled for Jose to come up to her and told him she wanted to save all 5 of them.

"But we are happy here," said Jose then he paused for a while, looked down to the ground feeling ashamed and continued, "sure, sometimes Vucinic screams at us or hits us but he's doing that to toughen us."

"No, Jose. These bad fellows just want you guys for their own benefit. They stole you from your families years or months ago. Do you still remember your parents or families?" Jamie asked, staring straight into Jose's eyes with her hands on his shoulders.

"Family? I don't think my parents even care about me," one of the boys retorted.

"Jose told us if they cared they would have come to get us by now. Besides, we're happy here. We belong here, Jose. Vulcinic is going to kill us if he finds us talking to her."

"No, come with me. I don't want you boys to grow up becoming one of them." Jamie tried to lure them by grabbing their emotions. "All of you have a bright future ahead of you. Come with me. I promise you, you will do much better."

"I'm not going," Jose said.

"Me neither," followed the other boys.

"If Jose' not going, we aren't either," confirmed Johnny, the youngest of the boys.

"Boys listen. Look at Jas, Douglas, Joe, and the rest. They were once like you guys. They were taken away from their parents and brainwashed to become one of those bad guys. Their whole lives' were robbed to become what they have become today. They can't turn back because they have become ransom. You, boys, have a whole future ahead, and I really don't want you to be at their mercy and eventually die in their hands," Jamie tried desperately to convince the kids. "I just want the best for all of you. I can't stand here waiting for you to decide, they will come looking for me soon. You guys with me or not?"

"I'm going to go with her," Jose told the rest.

"I don't even know how my parents look like. The only thing I know is my name. I can't even remember where my home is. It's been so long. You sure you can save us?"

"Positive!" Jamie assured them.

Then a voice calling for the boys came from a far, "Jose you little shit, where the fuck are you? Fuck even that bitch is missing."

Jamie grabbed Jose' and Joey's hands and led the rest out of the building as fast as they could. She was sure someone was going to start an extensive manhunt in a matter of minutes.

She managed to convince 4 of the 5 boys to run off with her as they kept heading further and further from the building as fast as their feet could take them. The directions from their location to NCSU in Raleigh were all locked up in her head as she led them through streets that were moderately crowded. That way they could all try walking at normal pace for fear that one of Rachel's people might be tailing them from behind any moment soon.

After heading up north, her worries transformed to a smile when she finally saw the NCSU building. They stopped at the foot of the building, Jamie caught her breath and instructed the boys, "I'll have to leave you all here. Now hurry up enter and seek help from them." Jamie pointed at the building entrance to the NCSU Police Department. "I've got to run for my own life now. Tell them everything, expose those people, Jas, Rachel, all of them. I hope you kids will eventually find your families."

"What about you, Carol?" asked Jose as he led the group of children towards the

NCSU building.

"These guys won't help me," Jamie shouted out as she looked towards the NCSU building, then started taking off at a quicker pace, "I've got to go. Now, take good care of yourselves ok? And tell them as much as possible about having been lured to abduction by those people."

Heart pounding, she took off on her own as she headed towards the Canadian Consulate in Raleigh to seek refuge along a moderately busy street.

As she fought exhaustion, her tired legs were trying hard to make their way as fast as possible to the consulate office, something warned her to keep a lookout for the perpetrators, she trusted her instincts and noticed from a glance, a car halted at the stop light to the east of where she was and spotted Vucinic pointing his gun at her. Before he could pull the trigger from afar, Jamie screamed and collapsed to the ground, attracting several passers-by to charge towards her. As Vucinic pulled over his car and was about to walk toward Jamie to kill her, a police car arrived. He immediately returned to his car to keep a close watch at the scene where Jamie was being surrounded. She woke up, scanned the faces in the crowd, and as soon as she spotted a police officer, she asked him to take her to the closest medical center citing the excuse that her head hurt. As she got escorted to the police car, she glanced at the direction where Vucinic had parked his car but noticed that he was gone. Only after she entered the police car that she picked up the courage to reveal her identity to the officer, explained that her belongings had been stolen and convinced them to send her to the Canadian Consulate in Raleigh safely instead of the medical center. She was careful not to disclose where she was heading to anyone in the crowd for fear someone might have been stopped by Vucinic along the way as the latter would have been interested to know where Jamie was heading.

FIFTY
Back On Track

As she made her way back to British Columbia and as the car approached closer to an atmosphere filled with familiarity, she saw her boys, Russell and his friends playing basketball outside her home while Raymond, the younger twin sitting by the steps of the patio looking upset. For a moment they stopped their game and turned their attention towards the slowing car as if they had been doing the same thing for the past year trying to keep a lookout for a missing person, their mom. Faces of curiosity immediately transformed to looks of relief as they abandoned their game, Raymond finally put a smile on his face as the both of them rushed towards the parked car to embrace their long lost mother, all three of them unable to control their tears of relief.

Jamie and her kids decided to relocate to Atlantic Canada to start a new life. A week before she left, she met her former colleague, Jonathan for a farewell lunch. She shared her entire ordeal with him, and as they walked out from the restaurant after their get together, she walked past a man sitting 2 tables next to theirs, his phone started ringing, she looked down and noticed the caller ID, which said Vucinic. That name sent chills down her spine as she looked straight into the man's eyes and recollected the same guy she had noticed the first time she had lunch with Jonathan almost a year back when they had a conversation about investing. She turned to Jonathan and caught a glimpse of her colleague nodding and smiling back at the same man. Perhaps it was Jonathan's friendly disposition or...could he be linked with the Syndicate? Jamie immediately became suspicious of her close friend who might be one of the accomplices to the biggest underground crime that has remained untouchable by law enforcement authorities. *Maybe that explains why he is one of the richest English teachers in Vancouver?* She thought to herself. *I really mustn't trust anybody anymore.*

For the safety of hers and her twins, they relocated to Ontario and assumed new identities. David decided to join them six months later. It took her almost two years to get part of her money stuck in Germany released back to her.

Throughout this journey, she had learned the powerful effects of storytelling and started a blog encouraging youths and adults to express themselves through stories incorporating coloring therapy and expressive writing. She hoped to cooperate with more social media users to continue her drive to create more awareness on the prevention of scams committed both on and offline, and someday to provide counseling to support victims with courage, hope, and sheer determination to live on.

Epilogue

They are everywhere - Some are standing right beside the innocent telling their stories even at this point while we're trying to find the true narrators of these engaging stories. Some of them are so effective at their job that they are able to suck in their audience's imaginations so well, the others are searching for new audience to share their stories with, while the rest are assisting behind the scene identifying what props to use next when their colleagues have identified and found their new audience.

As much as I hate to have to recall and relate this whole ordeal in detail, I know it is only right for me to do so especially living in North America, where scamming from organized syndicates has become the #1 unsolved crime in North America. The lack of collaboration between law enforcement authorities in these two countries has only encouraged this crime to spread ever so rampantly throughout North America, Canada, and parts of Europe and Asia. The annual revenues totaling over US$13billion in the year 2014 just from scamming victims in Canada, US, Europe and Asia combined has made this one of the most lucrative and successful businesses to operate on the planet.

I had been a target of scammers who profiled me via an online portal and fallen prey into their well-choreographed story. I became a victim of a horrible scam, and in the process, I was robbed off my identity as well. I lost an incredible amount of my savings as they manipulated my kindness and vulnerability at a time when I needed someone the most, which warranted the involvement of Interpol, the European and Asian authorities as the local RCMP or FBI couldn't assist much. It took me 2 hours to get out of the state of shock I was in that fateful day I discovered I was scammed, but I refused to surrender or to sink into despair or self-pity. Instead, my mind took over all the questions my heart was filled with that day. I decided to go all out to fight this battle and to subsequently offer assistance to other victims who have no one to turn to because not every victim could survive this ordeal on their own...not every victim would have the willpower to move on and rebuild their lives. Not every victim would want to tell their stories for fear of embarrassment, being judged and criticized for being gullible.

With all the hype we hear from the Americans about how effective their law enforcement authorities are, I wasn't surprised that up till today only the Australian authorities have made huge efforts to arrest these crooks despite the group scattered all over the world and not operating within the former's radar. The Australian authorities have even gone to the extent of collaborating with Nigerian and Malaysian authorities to capture a huge group of scammers from both countries.

Despite having gone through so many bureaucracies, the treatment I got from the RCMP and FBI, made my situation even more painful. An officer at my local division did take my report, but after much discussion with his department, I was told the crime occurred beyond their jurisdiction because money had been transferred out of the country. When I sent evidence which included fingerprints from a courier package the perpetrators had sent me, to the FBI from that state the postmark envelop had its stamp on, I was sent an email after much pursuit telling me I should only bring the matter up to the Internet Crime Complaint Center (better known as IC3) as well as the Canadian Anti Fraud Center and that the FBI or RCMP didn't have anything to do with this. That clearly indicated why scammers have been treating the US and Canada as one of their most lucrative playgrounds to boldly commit such criminal acts. They'd always manipulated the lax banking system in the US as money was transmitted from the victim to that account with not one bit of security measures taken by the US banking system.

It's time for law enforcement agencies as well as financial institutions from all over the world to get serious with this fraudulent tactics, unite and fight this crime together. Nailing down the syndicate requires a central agency assisted by a team of IT experts that should be dedicated to this problem as it is growing so rampantly. To make matters worse, these scamming activities are believed to contribute indirectly to funding terrorists groups. I've provided a lot of clues to the relevant authorities and much as I want to respect their privacy in handling the case, I don't believe they have taken whatever evidence and clues I've shared with them seriously because I kept my online dating profile active throughout the saga, only to encounter with yet the same group of perpetrators over and over again. I know they are still trying to scam new victims and trying to reach me via my Skype account but what really irks me is that the authorities are simply letting them continue with their 'scamming spree.' I was matched with an officer who happened to work for a law enforcement authority, and when I shared with him tips of the perpetrator from one of the dating sites, he just told me to report it to the vendor of the dating portal. The irony is the vendor of the dating portal actually instructed me to get the law enforcement officer to liaise with them in order for them to provide with the details of the perpetrators due to confidentiality and privacy agreement. This shows how slacken the bunch of authorities I have dealt with are at their jobs, they never seem to care despite having been showered with so many clues to capture the scumbags. They were given evidence containing fingerprints, IP addresses to track them and possibly set the scumbags a trap. They could have contacted the flower store that delivered the birthday flowers to me and to trace where the order had originally come from. The clues were many as they could even contact the software vendor, Magic Jack to obtain a list of IP addresses of those who had purchased that software. As the saying goes, where there is a will, there's obviously a way.

In this case, they could have done a lot more and not shut the door at me or any other victims' claiming that the crime didn't take place within their jurisdiction or that the value of our loss wasn't huge enough to warrant their attention to the case. If the Australian authorities could set a trap and nabbed a bunch of these scammers committing the crime freely in Malaysia or Nigeria, it really boils down to how dedicated our local authorities are towards solving the #1 unsolved crime that has been plaguing North America today. If global law enforcement authorities want to fight terrorism, they should step up and fight the root of the problem. This is the root of it all. This is one of the ways their syndicates use to fund their ruthless act of terrorism.

Each time someone reads about a new victim scammed, they judge and jump to conclusions that the victims were simply gullible or stupid. Instead of judging and drawing a conclusion from the twist of events that had taken place, I am sure anyone could have been a victim because these perpetrators always studied their prospective victims before jumping in to gain their trusts and eventually con them off their savings. They would only share stories and say things which their victims want to hear. Most victims don't discuss their ordeal because they worry their problems will distant them or reflect upon them - as if they are gullible or stupid to have been scammed. They end up struggling in silence, and that's how some end up feeling depressed or resort to ending their lives.

In my case, it did feel as though I had made a huge offering to the devils during the 7th month of the Chinese Lunar Calendar, who escaped from the gates of hell to disrupt my life as I was pretty vulnerable being a lonely, divorced woman, in my late 30s when all I really wanted was to find true love and a terrific partner who would complement my life and would love my kids as his own.

Having written this book inspired by my own true story turned out more of a catalyst as I learn to finally let go of what I had experienced. Although as I was writing some parts of the scam, I had to abandon writing the book for a couple of days to take a deep breath as the thought of what they did was painful and tough for me to digest. But I must admit the freedom that comes after letting it go, has finally allowed me to break free and live life beyond my wildest dreams.

www.ingramcontent.com/pod-product-compliance
Lightning Source LLC
Chambersburg PA
CBHW022127170626
46808CB00002B/880